This ROAD of MINE

Seosamh Mac Grianna
Translated by Mícheál Ó hAodha

THE LILLIPUT PRESS
DUBLIN

First published in Irish as *Mo Bhealach Féin* by An Gúm,
Baile Átha Cliath/Dublin, Ireland, 1940

This translation first published 2020 by
THE LILLIPUT PRESS
62–63 Sitric Road, Arbour Hill
Dublin 7, Ireland
www.lilliputpress.ie

ISBN 9781843517894

A CIP record for this title is available from
The British Library.

10 9 8 7 6 5 4 3 2

The Lilliput Press gratefully acknowledges the financial
support of the Arts Council/An Chomhairle Ealaíon.

Set in 10.5pt on 17pt Sabon by iota (www.iota-books.ie)
Printed in Spain by GraphyCems

FOREWORD

A hundred years ago Seosamh Mac Grianna (1900–90) was beginning his journey as a writer. Little bits and pieces of fiction and journalism in Irish were beginning to appear in print around the 1920s. Born in 1900 in Rann na Feirste, part of the Donegal Gaeltacht, Mac Grianna could not have imagined that a century later his work would still be read in Irish and, indeed, in translation in English. His active writing career was far too brief: fifteen years or so, from his early twenties until his mid-thirties. Ill health dogged him often through his days and he spent many long decades under care – his pen set aside.

Yet here we are, the fistful of books that he wrote and his journalism still attracting readers. The quality of what he created has trumped all: war, illness, anger, neglect and personal tragedy. There is a lesson there, perhaps, for all writers of Irish – indeed for all writers who do not work in English, who work in native languages, smaller languages, ancient set-aside languages, can still be rewarded with a dedicated readership; that original books can still cast a spell through the long decades; that imaginative, intelligent and thoughtful writing finds its place on book shelves and in the hearts and minds of loving readers.

Mac Grianna was a remarkable man and lived in remarkable times. He was born in Donegal at a time when the cataclysm of the Great Famine was still in living memory. His Donegal was part of a united Ireland, under the British Crown, at a time when the sun did not set on the British Empire. He saw the outbreak of the Great War and was tempted to join the British army but the Easter Rising set him on a different course. He saw the War of Independence and the Civil War that followed and **chose** the Republican – and losing – side. He saw partition draw a scar across Ulster and he saw native governments in Dublin try to give Irish an honoured place in a new, truncated Ireland.

He wrote during it all. There is no doubt that the times in which he lived informed the literature he produced. He knew the traditional lore of his townland and respected it, but often found his fiction in contemporary Ireland and its politics. In this, he was undoubtedly influenced by the writing and journalism of both Pádraic Ó Conaire (1882–1928) and Patrick Pearse (1879–1916).

The Irish language was his medium; the poor benighted, ignored, miraculous, mysterious Irish that was (and is) the community language of Rann na Feirste and much of Donegal even then. It was, and is still, a language of no commercial value; English was, and remains, the language of the powerful and influential. Irish is the echo of other times: of wars, conquest and famine, of events and of people who are not to be discussed in polite society. It was the language of the poor, of the most marginal and disdained.

Mac Grianna, however, found his voice and vision in the Irish language and embraced it. Irish was the harder choice for him, a language that places the writer into a very small circle of readers – and not that many native speakers could even read Irish in Mac Grianna's youth.

Still, it *is* an ancient language. That much is true. The writer of Irish may not enjoy the cachet of the English-language writer but, in these days of *A Game of Thrones*, the writer of Irish can, legitimately, point to legends in Irish that are every bit as fantastical, and brutal, as anything imagined by George R. R. Martin. The writer of Irish steps into a stream that stretches back thousands of years. Even in contemporary Ireland, a place that exists it seems only to buy and sell things, there are living Gaeltacht regions in all four provinces, battered and bruised, constantly under threat and endangered, but there nonetheless.

These Gaeltacht areas, like a shee fort, open up another Ireland and another Europe. These Gaeltacht regions light the way to Scotland, the Isle of Man, Wales, Cornwall and Brittany, to other linguistic realms that hint at a forgotten Europe and remind us of a different cultural past. Mac Grianna's journey took him to Wales and their Welsh language, a sister language to his own. There is curiosity in his travels around that land and a little envy perhaps that Welsh had seemed to survive in a way in which Irish had not. That country inspired one of his best books, *Mo Bhealach Féin* – a memoir and meditation.

Here we are then: still reading Mac Grianna's books a hundred years after he began his literary journey – in English however, a language he did not want to write in but a language whose naked power he understood. He translated much from English into Irish in an effort to earn much needed money. He knew the importance of the translator's role of turning the unfamiliar into the familiar, of presenting good literature to new readers.

Mac Grianna noted once that the poet's journey was a lonely one. It is, but you do meet friends on the way. I think he would be glad that a writer of conscience and creativity like Mícheál Ó hAodha has taken on this task on his behalf. Yes, I think he would have been pleased to know that another writer graced him with his care and attention and that his literary journey continues into another century, in another way.

Pól Ó Muirí, author of Seosamh Mac Grianna:

Míreanna Saoil *(2007)*

Lá Fhéile Muire san Fhómhar, 2020

1

They say the truth is bitter, but believe me it's harsh and this is why people avoid it.

It was early in my life that I saw it stretched out in front of me, the road of my heart's desire, the winding path skirted by peaks more beautiful than any hills found in music and the breath of wind above more perfect than any earthly breeze – as wine vanquishes water; the old bridge that listens to the whispering stream for as long as first, fleeting memories linger; and whitewashed villages set between the early noon and the mouth of the dawn; and sheltered nooks quiet and peaceful where one rests and comes to know every living sprig and herb, the scattered roses made of dreams:

> *Ar bhruach na toinne le taobh na Finne*
> *'S mé 'féachaint loingis ar sáile.*

On the edge of the wave beside the Finn
As I looked on ships upon the sea.

The way of no return, that inconstant road between care and fear. Who'll tell me that I never walked it – me, the king of Gaelic poets in this, the twentieth century, the era of Revival? Who'll tell me that I was guided by the words of casual friends most days since I was born? And even if I was always slow to let them guide me, I still found myself halfway between admiration and contempt. You'd need patience with the likes of me, and I'll tell you now why. And I'm afraid they still won't understand even when I give them the truth straight.

But then, what's the point of me writing this here book if I am to remain misunderstood? And so I'll tell you now why I didn't keep my distance from these casual friends of mine the most of my days, and why I didn't take the path of joy and enchanted wandering as I should have; it's a long time now since I abandoned the armour that most other men sport – a steady job and opinions that stand to you and ensure you fit in with the crowd. Bad as I was, I never had any time for all of that. But then I also had a deep and powerful fear of myself. No wonder – when you think that my own crowd were always down on me as if there was a danger in me that the world could never see. And it was always like this: when someone else caught a cold, they felt sorry for them; if I got one, it was something to be ashamed of however. If someone else got angry, they were alright because they knew how to control themselves; but if I got angry, I was a wild bull of a man. If someone else did something untoward, it was quickly forgotten and they got away with it; but if I did something wrong, I never heard the end of it. I don't like this type of Christianity, if Christianity it is – but there's a lot of it in this world. Maybe I had a power in me that I didn't understand; maybe I still don't understand it. Is it any wonder that I felt myself tied up in a thousand knots before I'd done anything at all, I ask you? I rebelled. I broke out of schools and colleges. In 1916, I left Saint Eunan's with the intention of joining the British Army but Easter Week put an end to that. I disappeared from other colleges too and yet, despite it all, I reached the age of twenty-one and I had qualified as a schoolteacher. If it wasn't that I had some bit of guidance from others, if it wasn't that I had a right fear of myself, the truth is that I'd have had no education at all. They didn't understand what drove me deep down and even if they tried to give me the odd bit of guidance, it was only very rarely. I knew early on that they were trying to break my spirit in reality, and so I was rash and uncontrollable as a consequence. I was wary of others. I also wrote stories that might never have seen print if it wasn't for others. Because I've never believed that the poet should prostitute his art. Once my writing became known and others understood I had that gift which was very rare in the Ireland of my day – the gift of poetry – I think they expected me to share my store with them. I refused however. They couldn't get a word out of me. I never revealed what was really on my mind. I pro-tected my inner soul. People close to me claimed that I was lazy and yet the same people saw me working, and working harder than any man at times. They tried to pin me down and box me in but they could never manage it. I had too many sides to me. That's my gift. And eventually they let me be, even if they – my casual friends that is – kept inviting me around to their houses for longer than I'd hoped. In the end, they left me alone. It was painful at first but I got used to it. Because I always wanted to be alone. There were people close to me that I had a great respect for needless to say – in so far as they understood. But I could tell that they wanted too much from me and even if I'd shared my gifts with them from morning till night and week on week, they'd never have been satisfied. Maybe I made them jealous or greedy.

Maybe I didn't understand then what I do now – that it's in our nature to steal the wealth – one man from the next. I hope I never hurt anyone. To put twenty words into one, for the guts of ten years I tried to make a living the same as anyone else, even if any blind man born could tell that I wasn't like the others. I was afraid back then that if I found myself in trouble no one would help me out. And it's in my nature that I couldn't care less about anyone else. A searing honesty and courage is what lies behind this view of the world. I always knew – because I've got a wise head on me – that honesty is very difficult if you're too poor for it and the same goes for courage also. You can make the most of your gifts if you have a bit of material comfort. But because I didn't give a damn about humanity, I found myself on the margins. Still, my imagination and art were well served by this isolation seeing as I was free of the pollution of the mind that characterizes contact with others. Life has a grip on every man born in one essential aspect however. People may differ from one another but they all have an appetite and I had an appetite as good as the next man. I had to keep my belly full. I had to earn my bread somehow; and the wheat can't grow by itself.

I won't bother here now with the nine schools I taught in across the nine counties of Ireland. Or the fact that I gave up teaching in the end when I had a dream that the whole world was bound tight with ropes – up, down and across – like the lines in a school roll-book. I couldn't suffer the world any longer and it embroidered this way. The second job I had was translating books into Irish. The government was running a scheme for the publication of Irish-language books and I began working on this. Not that the government of the day was known for its promotion of poetry or art. And the truth is, neither I nor the others were too taken with An Gúm¹ from the beginning either – other than making jokes about it, that is. It came looking for me and gave me books to translate. An Gúm had a welcome for everyone back then, or until it had enough books published to keep it up and running. But then the publisher became difficult and it was afraid that people might earn big money from it. We won't bother with that for the moment however. The way I saw it – it was willing to pay me for work that was as easy as tying your shoelaces, so that I didn't give a damn what the place was called really or what stupidity it got up to either.

I wasn't long working there however when I discovered that this business was no game – not at all. I was working with literature the same way another man cuts timber or collects sawdust. An Gúm were the harshest people on writing

I've ever come across and even if six or seven of the greatest poets that ever lived came back and worked for them, they couldn't have been harsher or more strict on them. There were others working there also whose company I often found myself keeping. But it was just my luck that any time we met up the sole topic of conversation was An Gúm. It was bad enough working in the place but to be talking about it all the time as well! I'd run into people I knew every now and then out on the street and they'd ask me: 'Are you still translating the books into Irish?' That was a real punch in the gut for me, you can be sure, the likes of me who'd proved that I could write real poetry! I hated An Gúm and it was this same hatred that kept the few small embers in my soul aflame – until it came time for the reckoning. I always hoped to destroy An Gúm somehow and I couldn't have cared less about the consequences for myself either. This is not to say that there weren't some advantages to working there of course. I didn't have to get up too early in the mornings or rush around the place like everyone else. And I got my wages in a lump sum and enjoyed spending it too. But then I was tied down in other ways also. I never trusted the civil servants in the system fully. I took the advice of my casual friends and didn't get above my station either – by earning more money than others or by making waves at work. I watched and learned how the world works quietly and in my own way instead. And I loved the freedom of working there even if I was tied down by certain rules and regulations in other ways also. It was still much better than the slave whose every hour is subject to the clock.

I was four years working there when the government changed. This was likely the moment of reckoning, I said to myself. It was just after New Year in 1932. A few of us did whatever we could to find out what the future held for us there. People went and spoke to the newly appointed Minister. Articles appeared in *An Phoblacht*[2] criticizing An Gúm in case what was being done 'through the official channels' wasn't enough. We did our best – or as best we could – given the circumstances. I was happy to continue working there as things stood. But the others wouldn't listen to me. We weren't all pulling together, not at all. I have my suspicions that one man was trying to get a job in An Gúm while another was afraid of his life that he'd be kept on, and a few others didn't care one way or the other, and there was me just left on my own really.

The story I had in with the publisher – *An Droma Mór*[3] – was different from the usual stuff they published. And there was no way I'd give them the satisfaction of rejecting it, I told myself. So I went down to the office one day and took the book away again with me. Maybe they'd never seen someone angry in that office before, but they saw me raging that day, that's for sure. I don't remember everything I said to them but anyway I asked for the manuscript back and was forced to grab the man who had it by the scruff of the neck and half-throttle him in the end. And I was delighted that I did this too. Because if I'd spent much longer in An Gúm translating books to Irish, I wouldn't have had a spark of creativity left in me. Sure, I'd have had a way of making a living alright but I'd have been like someone who'd neither won nor lost – just a boring machine, an automaton. I lost out on the cushy number, cursed though it was, but at least I was free to go my own road. And it's not as if I passed the rest of my days without tasting the better nectar of life either. I put myself in harm's way and even in mortal danger many a time – ever since that afternoon when I jumped into seven feet of water on a remote beach without a safety ring, and I just ten years of age. When the fighting broke out in 1920 I was involved in it to a certain extent. I didn't understand what it was all about of course – but that's another story. Because, in truth, we in the Donegal Gaeltacht were never completely colonized. As far back as 1602, Rory O'Donnell had destroyed his pursuers at Cornaslieve and Beltra after the Battle of Kinsale and the English made peace with him. If he'd been beaten, he'd have been put to death. We still have most of the noble families in the Donegal Gaeltacht to this day, something that can't be said about any other Gael-tacht. And I know that the Brehon Laws are still followed on strictures relating to the raising of sheep in my native parish even today. So, I spent a while in prison for a cause that I hadn't the slightest interest in really. This taught me a bit about life even if it numbed my emotions and creativity in many other ways as well. The likes of us are as strangers amongst the anglicized Irish. Reflecting on this now, various notions come to mind: how we were forbidden as children from calling a woman a fool – or saying that someone was ugly or a liar. We received the education of the nobility espe-cially in Aileach,[4] the place where the Gaels held most power in ancient times. The most wonderful thing of all is how the racehorse is better beneath the plough than the heavy nag. Even if our people are quieter and more even-tempered, this doesn't mean that they don't do Trojan work and suffer hardship that would break people anywhere else. We can't avoid the truth however and we must suffer it. Seeing as I've brought the discussion around to it, I too have survived many hardships over the years and benefited by them also. I wasn't following my own road fully when I endured them however. What I would really love to do is turn the world upside-down so that there was magic in every living thing even if it was only scratching yourself. Indeed, I'd say that you're probably not allowed scratch yourself anymore the way things are these days. But says I to myself: Hey An Gúm! I'm off to follow my own road now and without your permission either!

2

I was staying in quite a big lodging house at this time. It was a busy place with lots of people coming and going including newspaper-men and couples from the country who'd got married in the city; there were lots of them there. I met people from all over – from Norway to Australia. Funnily enough, the most interesting character of the lot was the woman who ran the lodgings itself. She had Jewish blood, I think, and she was dark and had an unusual swarthy look about her that would have put you in mind of a city when the night is over. Although she was middle-aged she used to plaster herself in make-up as if all she had in mind was hunting men. She was married to a decent and very polite man whom she'd cursed with bad luck by all accounts. She was hard-working, worldly and greedy and, that said, she was a poet.

In hindsight, I can see now that my stint in that lodgings was as nice as it was in any of the twenty-five lodging houses I stayed in from my first arrival in Dublin. I had a small room upstairs at the very top of the house, four floors up, and I did my writing in the sitting room at the window, looking out at the park across the way. This sitting room was crowded with people sometimes, especially at night, when I sat there writing and between every second sentence I'd listen in on the chat going on around the fire.

The lodging-house woman had a son of whom it would be untrue to say that he was his father's son in any way – a man who was as fascinating as herself. He was a big, heavy lad whose black hair was streaked with grey. They regularly made out that he was only twenty-two but he looked at least thirty-five, if he was a day. He had a religious mania as strong as I've seen in any man and all he ever talked about was religion. He was a teacher but he wanted to leave his job and join one of the religious orders. He'd arrive into the room eager for a chat every afternoon and before I knew it we'd be debating everything religious. He had a whole host of stories about the bodies of saints that had remained uncorrupted for hundreds of years, stories that I didn't believe at all. These weren't the type of stories that I'd heard tell of growing up in the Gaeltacht at all and it often got me thinking that the Catholic faith in the Gaeltacht and in the areas outside it was very different. I can't remember many of our conversations now but one image that remains clear in my mind is the sight of this man's dark, fleshy face and his grey-flecked hair and the tormented soul that was him. And his mother told me herself that he was always keen on joining one of the religious orders but that it'd break her heart if he did.

She'd lost a son already in the Great War of 1914. There was no question but that she and the son were mad about each other; there was just them in the world. Her daughter was always cleaning and cooking from morning till night and her husband spent all his time down in the kitchen, and to tell you the truth I don't know whether he was washing dishes or what he was doing. Any time she left the house for a walk, it was the son who went with her and whenever she went to the pictures he was with her too. He went with her the same whenever she went on holidays. They were the gentry of the family – no doubt about it.

This woman often called in to me for a chat about her son and the poetry that she wrote. She regularly gave me newspapers – the local ones – to read also. There's a 'poet's corner' in these newspapers and not a week went by that this woman's compositions weren't in the newspaper. She'd been living in the district that this newspaper covered before she'd first come to live in Dublin city.

There are many different schools of poetry in the English language, but I don't know of one that would describe this woman's work. Her poems were a little bit similar to those of Mrs Hemans, the ones we'd had in our schoolbooks long ago. I'm not sure whether I can give the reader a flavour of her writing but this translation may give you a sense of it:

You were with me on my journey each day,
For many long years you were my love;
Many is the tale that you heard
If only you could tell them again today

When I was young and you by my side
I was not without pride and my heart was not heavy;
I used to walk the road to the town,
Everybody said I'd a sweet way about me.

But old age came in the same way as night falls,
And it left both me and you lamenting;
You are worn out now, without value or beauty –
My little old satin bag I myself had.

She thought that the ending to the poem was very clever
and that everyone assumed that she was lamenting a lover or
a friend up to that point. She told me about stories that she
wanted to write one day if only she had the opportunity. She
had some sort of a love story about people living in a castle in
France but if I was to be hanged now I can't remember it. She
said she had another story that would amaze the world if she
wrote it. She'd never write it however in case it put someone
in mind of committing a terrible deed. This was a story about
a woman who hated her husband so much that she wanted
him dead. The woman began giving him damp shirts regularly until he fell sick and died. But there wasn't a law in the
world that could prove she'd killed him. She was afraid some
woman might do something similar if she wrote the book.
But what I was afraid of – in my own mind – was that she
might do it herself to her own husband seeing as she detested
him so much. I stayed in that lodgings for the winter and
many people came and went during that time. I had a visit
up at the top of the house one day that was different from
most however. A messenger came to me from the firmament

just as I was going to sleep one night. I was looking deep into my own soul when a dove appeared and stood on my windowsill. It was like a messenger from another world, a world vast and boundless, and hidden from us, a perilous realm that sought to draw you in – like beautiful music far away in the enchanted fairy sphere. If you spotted a dove sitting on your windowsill in a lit-up room very late at night you'd know what I mean. You couldn't but take note of its eyes, feral and untamed, its striking plumage; and you too would feel the living tremble of its tiny body. You wouldn't have paid any heed to this same bird if you'd spotted it out in a field or on a background framed by leaves – but all that was here now was a tiny room, bare and empty except for a bed, a press, and one small cheap picture – and a wall plastered in paper – the most unnatural sight that man ever created. But in that moment, my little room, shabby yet cosy, was extinguished as if in a flash of light or torn apart by a great gust of sea-wind. And I saw a thousand leagues of sky in that dove's eyes and a thousand enclosed cities and eddying rock-pools beneath me, and I was king of eternal wind and sky.

Whether it was by nature or education, my first instinct was to try and catch that dove somehow. This was when that room turned small and narrow however, so narrow that the poor dove panicked and flew crazily all over the place and it would have killed itself only that I managed to get the window open. It shot out across the street in three flaps of its wings and came to rest on a tree opposite. That winged dart of his – as noble and magnificent as a wave – has remained with me ever since, as mournful as a wound.

The people of the house told me the history of that dove later. It had belonged to an army captain who'd lodged there at one time. They asked me whether I'd noticed the ring on its leg and sure enough, it had sported a ring alright. The captain had moved from that lodgings eventually and he had left that part of his life behind – whether it was that he'd got married or had died or been imprisoned, or whether he'd just gone to live somewhere else, I don't know. But his dove had returned there every now and then, visiting that top window as if to pay tribute to the old captain.

This was my way too, I thought, this same wild appearance and retreat. I too would love to have disappeared through the top window the same as the dove, particularly seeing as I owed ten pounds in rent. I'm as honest a man as walks the Western world, I think, but when it comes to money, it's not much of a crime to leave a lodging-house woman ten pounds short when you've paid her a year's rent. Anyway, I didn't have the ten pounds to give her and there's no law for necessity. I began to pack my bits and pieces together carefully one day and made ready to escape. If you think for one minute however that this woman didn't sense what I was up to, then you're asleep in this world! Like the dog who gets the scent of the rabbit, she was onto me immediately and knew that I was up to something. Once I'd my bag packed, I went down to dinner and she was over to me straight away.

'Mac Grianna,' she says, 'I'm waiting on that ten pounds from you. I've bills to pay you know.'

'My good woman,' I says, 'I know exactly what you mean. Shur, we all have bills to pay but as the good Prayer says:

"Forgive us our trespasses as we forgive those who trespass against us." As I gently informed you previously, I don't get paid by the week and I've to wait a good while sometimes before my money comes through. You gave me leeway on paying my debts before and I'm sure you'll do it again.'

'That's alright,' she says, 'but you should know that it doesn't suit me to keep lodgers that don't pay me every week. I've a lot of expenses on this house. I'll expect that money from you come the end of the week.'

'Alright,' I says. 'You'll have it by the end of the week even if I've to sell the shirt off my back. Don't worry love. I won't let you down. I know you've enough things to be worrying about as it is never mind getting paid on time.'

I saw her off from the door of my room but only just about. She spent the rest of the day sniffing around. I went into the sitting room and hunched over a book and you wouldn't have known (unless you were the lodgings-woman, that is) that I planned on running – no more than the leaving of Carraig Dun.[1]

The next day I waited until I saw her leaving the house all dressed up. Rather than leave it too late, you better go for it now, I says to myself and I ran upstairs, as alert and quick as the cat pursuing the bird. Back in the room, I realized that I hadn't packed my bag right at all and that I'd left out the most important things. I pulled the bag open and threw in whatever I could. But like all the bags of the world, I couldn't get it to close for me there and then. This was bad enough but I couldn't even curse the bloody thing rightly while I was at it! I gave it one mighty push and eventually managed to get it closed, then stuck my head outside the door. The house was so quiet that I heard myself tremble and it felt as if a full hour passed before I negotiated the first flight of stairs and scanned the doors below – it felt so long. And if the sun outside hadn't told me otherwise, I'd have a sworn a week went by before I reached the ground floor. I was just a few steps from the front door when the sitting room door opened and who appeared all of a sudden but herself! And there was me thinking that the boss-woman must be a least a mile away by then! Who'll deny that lodgings-women have magic powers all of their own?

'Hey! Hey!' she says and she rightly wound-up! 'You're not leaving until I get what I'm owed!'

'Hang on! Hang on!' I says. 'I don't owe you anything and don't think you're going to stop me leaving either! No man will stand in my way, I swear,' I says, trying to push past her.

'Hey, Cyril!' she says. 'Hey, Cyril!'

And where was the son but right outside the front door ready to block my escape. He put his hand on the glass of the front door and pushed his way in, then grabbed a hold of my bag. In that instant, and as clear as day I saw them – every tasteless drop of tea and every miserly slice of bread and every pretence of a dinner I'd ever had – in all twenty-five lodging houses – they flashed through my mind all at once. All the suffering and loneliness of those places rose up inside me like one powerful wave and I clocked that righteous, grey-streaked buck with an almighty punch. I hit him so hard that I thought I'd broken all the bones in my hand and he crumpled onto the ground as if he'd been pole-axed stone-dead. I jumped out the door and made a run for it. I went around the corner at the top of the road and kept running and if I was followed, I didn't see anyone. Then I slowed to a walk. I wasn't long convincing myself that I'd killed that man however and that I'd left him dead on the side of the road behind me and that I was in deep trouble. I was sure too that guilt was written all over my face and that anyone who passed by could see it clear as day. And I was sure that people were avoiding my gaze, it was so obvious. At one stage, I spotted a big, tough-looking guard across the street and I was sure that he'd recognized me and so I slipped around the corner as fast as a weasel through a ditch.

I wasn't stupid of course and I knew that they couldn't hang me for punching your man back there but seeing as I was on the run, I was as well letting on to myself that I'd killed a man and that the human race were bent on revenge and pursuing me for justice. Suddenly, as if from nowhere, a lodging house appeared ahead on the road and it reminded me – despite my best intentions – that I'd just killed someone. It had the look of a place that a killer might hide out in. It was off the beaten track and looked as if no one ever stayed there and even if I was fairly well-up on all the streets in that part of the city – so much so that I knew half of the people around there to see – I'd never noticed this lodgings before. The name of the place was written above the door in big brass letters, half-broken and missing, so that one could say with absolute truth that it was a house without a name. I went in. A sullen, dark-looking girl appeared after a few minutes from somewhere in the back and I asked for lodgings. She handed me an old ledger to write my name in, a ledger so ancient looking that you'd have sworn no one had written in it since the Book of Promises. In for a penny, in for a pound, I thought and signed myself in as 'Cathal Mac Giolla Ghunna' [Charles McElgun].[2] I'd convinced myself by then that there was a dead man after me for sure.

I spent that evening sitting in a big, wide room made of a poor light and a terrible loneliness. No one came in or out except for two or three people who looked like university students. They sat themselves over on the far side of the room so that they might as well have been a quarter of a mile away as far as I was concerned. I glanced over at them the odd time thinking: if you only knew the terrible deed I've just committed! And sure enough, it wasn't long before I could tell they'd marked me down as a bit odd, and so I hid my face from them as best I could. I tried to put together a plan then on how best to evade the enemy in pursuit, but couldn't think of anything. I just couldn't focus on the task in hand. All I could think of was my pursuers and I felt sure that the guards were looking for me already. They were most likely on their way to the lodgings right then. In fact, they were probably outside the door waiting for me to appear. They'd arrest me and they'd have a great story to tell, and they'd have a long life and success and I'd have the exact opposite. Every now and then I glanced over at the door to see if there was any commotion out on the landing and then back again at the young people sitting over at the table. Eventually, they went out of the room and left me by myself. I didn't stay long sitting in that shadow-filled room however. Everything in it was battered and broken and the place had a mournful look about it. The chairs were bent and twisted, there was no fire, and there was a clock above the hearth that had said three o'clock for the guts of twenty years. A small statue of a Greek god stood next to the clock and one of its legs was broken and all you could say about it was: 'How the mighty have fallen!'

There was something poetic about the room all the same – if you'd just walked into a comedy sketch perhaps ... But once the desolation of the room had infused me, I'd had enough of it. I'll go up to my room, I thought, and watch the flow of the streets outside, and reflect on what I've done that day. Up there, I says, I'll put what I did to the blessed grey-streaked lad into perspective – that fellow I thought peculiar and whom I'd left stretched on the ground after me like a corpse. I went upstairs and sat at the window and smoked for a while. If it wasn't for the tobacco, I'd never have survived. I'd have lost it years ago. I'd have gone stir-crazy and torn the whole place up – everything from Odhráin's Great House[3] to the Rif Mountains[4] far away. God strike me down if I tell a lie! I looked out into the street, even if there wasn't anything very interesting outside! Just people walking past, some of them silent and some of them talking. There was a hotel directly across from me and a man was standing at the door as if waiting for someone. A bright glare of light came from inside and it looked as if they were hosting a dinner or a meeting of some kind in there. There was something absurd about the hotel, and the entire street, in truth. It was as if children had constructed the entire city – small, simple people who'd never have survived in the real world at all, if it wasn't that others were out there breaking in the ground and the slopes of the hills for them and working the land, people who were kind to children. A second thought struck me then however – they were only letting on with this childish frivolity and foolishness of theirs and there was something sinister and dangerous in them – behind it all. I sensed that the city people were the enemy now and that they were all united in revenge on me for killing the blessed grey-streaked fellow back there. My thoughts began to race and I said to myself that I'd have to leave that place soon and hide myself away somewhere as best I could for a while.

There's no better way to delay your pursuers and put them off the scent than to give them plenty to think about, I thought. If I was walking on sand now, and they were after me, I'd leave no traces and they'd lose my trail. And whatever few tracks I'd leave, I'd put strange twists and turns into every footprint so they wouldn't know whether I was drunk or crazy, or just totally lost, and eventually I'd walk into the sea and swim a mile back to where I'd originally left the shore. And I'd change my clothes and my name again and between tram, train and bus, I'd circuit the city until I was back close to where I'd left in the first place. Such thoughts put me at my ease and I fell asleep. I've always had a great interest in dreams and I was only asleep a short while I think, when a dream of sorts woke me up. But the images in this dream weren't as vivid or clear as usual however. I think my mind had been too alive during the day. I was tired however and I slept soundly because there's nothing that tires the body as much as the workings of the mind. I woke in the morning and I was staring out at the fine, bright day for a few minutes before I even remembered that I'd killed the blessed grey-streaked lad at all. I got up and made breakfast and then I went out and bought a new suit. It was summer and a fashionable suit wasn't too expensive but then I realized for the first time ever how difficult it is to hide something even in the big city. I didn't know where to get rid of the old suit. I checked out every hidey-hole and corner in that lodging house but none of them would do the job. I scanned the streets nearby to see was there any ragged-looking young lad I could give the suit to as a present. But then I thought that this might look a bit dodgy and I had to be careful. Eventually, I remembered the three brass balls above the pawnshop two streets away and the words 'Cash Office' written above the door in big letters like one of those offices belonging to the government that are so official they're reluctant to state their name in full. This wasn't the first time I'd been in a pawnshop either, I'd left in my jacket to one before and for the next fortnight I'd lived like a prince and had a fistful of money in my pocket – until I retrieved the suit again, that is.

I didn't know this particular shop and that was probably for the best. Down I went. Behind the counter was a heavy-jowled man who gave me a dubious look.

'How much?' he says.

I was never good at dealing with shop people. I'm always afraid that my two eyes say it straight out: 'Go to hell, you twopenny beggar.'

My people never owned shops; maybe they were too poor but there's something behind their pride all the same.

I'm certain that the blood of the free families runs strongly through my veins anyway: Dalys and Boyles and Gallaghers. And The Book of Invasions⁵ says that one of the Mac Griannas was king of Ireland when the Milesians first arrived to our shores.

'A pound,' I says.

'A half-a-crown,' he says.

'Between half-a-crown and a pound,' I says.

'Three shillings,' he says.

'Alright,' I says. 'She's best staying here with you now anyway as she's too worn out for me to hang onto anymore.'

'What name?' he says.

'Art Mac Cumhaidh.'⁶

'What address?'

'Úir-Chill an Chreagáin,' I says in a low voice.

'What's that?' he says.

'The Speckled-House Hotel.'

'Never heard of it,' he says.

'It's at the corner of Such-and-Such a Street,' I added.

As I was leaving the shop again, I saw him call over a boy and say something to him. He's sending a messenger out now with a note to 'The Speckled-House Hotel', I said to myself. I hopped on a bus as quickly as I could and it brought me out to the south side of the city. I got off halfway, returned through a back street, hopped on a tram and returned to the city again. I hopped off the tram halfway in and went into a pub that was off the main thoroughfare. I ordered a bottle of beer and took out a newspaper I'd bought and began reading. I searched through the advertisements for lodgings and found one that was suitable. But the type of person who's used to reading a lot – the likes of me – only scans things really and doesn't bother reading anything fully unless it really grabs their attention, and of course, there's not much poetry in ads for lodging houses. I pulled out a pen to mark the page. Then a strange thought came to me. If I mark this now and suppose my enemies get their hands on this newspaper somehow, I'll be caught. Maybe I could mark it with beer. I put a drop of beer on it and marked it but then I was afraid that once dried, the mark might disappear. So I marked the edge of the paper, in the margin, three columns over. Once I'd finished drinking the beer, I went straight back to the lodgings. I had a head start and I took it. After I was three or four days there, and there was no sign of anyone looking for me, I knew well by then that I hadn't killed that grey-streaked fellow at all and I felt a bit embarrassed about the whole thing. I wasn't so much of a big man really after all, was I? – seeing as I hadn't killed that fellow when I had the chance? What was the point of travelling my own road if there was no memorial erected to me one day – so as the next person coming along could read it and say they'd never seen a man the likes of me before. The fact that I'd left no legacy behind me annoyed me so much that I felt like walking out into the city right then and killing the first person I came across. But to hell with the Dublin people anyway. When someone's quiet and calm and easy-going, they're as nasty and vicious as a bunch of weasels but when someone's ready to smash their head in, they're as gentle and meek as lambs.

3

Once I was settled in new lodgings I began considering how best to make a living. I remember thinking that if I'd had a cave somewhere out in the Wicklow Mountains I could have survived by stealing sheep and potatoes and twenty other things. I saw myself as clear as day stretched out and relaxing on my sheepskin rug and no jealousy or badness from others to bother me. This thought fixated me so much that I went over to the library and checked out some maps of where best to make my hideout and I was between two minds whether Glenmalure or the Sally Gap was best. It'd be important to be near water and as close as possible to a food supply, but far away from people's prying eyes at the same time. Examining the map, I realized just how little wilderness was left in Ireland as a whole at this stage and how little land exists that isn't surrounded by ditches and fences and someone keeping a close and envious eye on it. Even if you'd had the free-holding for a small sea island itself!

I forgot the whole idea about Wicklow a few days later and if anything good came out of it at all, it was the realization of how poor this country really is. Next, I thought of putting an ad in the paper – the likes of this:

> *Man, 30, strong, healthy and very energetic. More learned than most literary doctors. Nothing in the world that he can't do a brilliant job of – in his own way – and twenty other jobs he can't do better than they're usually done.*

No sooner had I this written but I thought to myself – there's no one in the world would respond to an ad like this. No one would hire someone the likes of this either. I had no choice but to remain destitute. I understood that much by now. I wasn't for sale to the highest bidder. Only slaves are for sale. I had to fend for myself.

I had no land and no money to set up a business however. I could go out collecting pennies on the street but I sensed the harvest was very poor. Or I could be a highwayman like Redmond O'Hanlon[1] in the good old days. I wandered around the city and checked out all the places where there was money and I wasn't long realizing that you needed time and planning to undertake a big robbery and you might be six months watching a place and waiting for your chance. I observed people rather than places next. But the rich all had cars and anyone I came across who was as out of it as I was, chances were that if I managed to rob their purse, they were as poor as myself.

I considered politics next. I'd never had much interest in politics for the simple reason that I wasn't that interested in people. It'd be a good thing to be in charge of Ireland, I thought, but if I got that far, I'd hang a lot of people and make slaves of many others. Because plenty of people deserved that, I said to myself, and I knew the difference between black and white only too well. I was thinking that I'd set up a Gaelic regime in Ireland and anyone who didn't have Irish – I'd make them a plough-man, a deliveryman or a slave of some description. I did attend one or two political meetings alright to see what was going on but once I found out that I'd have to do all the work myself, I put that idea on the backburner for some other time.

Eventually, my money started running out and I put an ad in the newspaper offering Irish-language classes. Not that teaching Irish was something I'd ever enjoyed much. Anyone brought up speaking English wouldn't understand what I mean by this. But if someone with good English had to teach it to people who had really bad English, they'd know exactly what I mean. Learners of Irish always reminded me of labourers who work with their hands, all blistered and raw. I'd a feeling too that some strange people would show up to learn from me.

I never had a hunch that didn't prove true either because only a few people responded to me, just one of whom was worth knowing. This was Tom Kerrigan. He was just eighteen years old yet wise beyond his years. And he had all the cuteness and nerve lads that age have. It was easier to teach Irish to Tom than any of the others but after he'd come to

me a few times for classes, I stopped teaching him Irish altogether. We both had lots of other things going on. We were
both observing and exploring the world to see where we
could find a niche or a chance for ourselves. I was older than
him of course and I knew that I'd have to make a mark on
the world sooner rather than later, while Tom had all the
optimism of youth about him and could still spot a chance
where I couldn't.

He was good at thieving. There are lots of lads around
these days who are well-up on thieving and breaking into
houses was Tom's favourite subject of conversation. At one
stage, we'd identified a certain house on the south side of the
city that we were going to break into. I thought of a different plan at the last minute however. I was good at reading
human nature. I can look at someone's face and body language and even read their hands as well. I don't know where
I acquired this skill from but I thought I could make money
out of it anyway. I told Tom this idea of mine.

'You'd make money, for sure,' he says. 'You should put
an ad into one of the papers saying: "Seosamh Mac Grianna,
telling fortunes for a shilling a go."'

'Hang on,' I says. 'Would this fellow be better off having
a Middle Eastern name?'

'He would,' he says.

'And he'd need to be famous all over the world. Let's see
now.'

'Sorry,' Tom says, 'I forgot something and I've to go home
quickly now for it.'

'Alright,' I says. 'I'll see you tomorrow.'

I wrote the ad out that night. This is it. I have it here on the table in front of me right now:

STARTLING!!!
ELI BEN ALIM
says your future can be foretold, and that of your lover, your child, and your friend in trouble.

ELI BEN ALIM, Arab prophet, knows the future as the skilled pilot knows the hidden rocks and the safe anchorages. He has travelled the five continents, has given readings for GENERAL WILLIAMSON, U.S.A., and for M. HENRI BEAUVAIS, famous French actor, the MAHATMA GANDHI, and the ex-King of Bulgaria.

Send ELI BEN ALIM a frank account of your problems. Give sex, date of birth. Enclose P.O. value 1s. 2d., or stamps.

Address............

'Do people the likes of this really exist?' Tom asks when I showed the ad to him.

'Now, that's a very big question!' I says. 'It'd be a right low-breed who refused to believe in the existence of Gandhi, and the king that lost Bulgaria. As for the other two, I've never heard anything about them – but the chances are that they're real people. As for Eli Ben Alim himself, don't you see him right here in front of you?'

'That's a brilliant ad,' he says. I know a man who'd type it up for you.'

I put the ad into various newspapers and anyone who's meticulous enough to go through the old papers, they'll find it still. And the things that I was told that season were never heard by another living soul – even the priests themselves in the confession box never heard the likes of it. Women, women, women and so many men that it'd shock you. I always knew that if you wanted to make an idiot of yourself you'd have plenty of people in this world to keep you company. And I got so many letters that Tom couldn't keep up with the clerical work on them. It was hard enough to read the handwriting sometimes but we had to decipher what we could from the letters. This was the only way I had to deduce anything about the person who'd written the letter. Many's the time I wrote the likes of this in my notes: 'You have black hair, you're reasonably tall and when walking you lead with the left foot and follow with the right.' Once I knew something about someone, I'd tell their fortune. It was good training for the mind and I'm sure that if I'd stayed at it long enough, I'd have made a good fortune-teller. I received too many letters however and I had no choice then but to write one general answer that I sent out to everyone. This is how most work is done these days anyway; when you're in contact with so many people at the one time, you don't have any time to get to know them, and you've to treat them all the same. And I'm a poet and I don't believe in wasting time on slog-work. I wasn't sure either when some anxious girl might pay me a visit and realize that I had neither the skin colour nor the rig-out of a prophet from the land of sand.

Eli Ben Alim disappeared from Ireland that winter and I was left high and dry as there was never much money in teaching Irish. But you don't need an awful lot to keep breath in your body and people are really alive only when they're living on very little. I was as good a customer as the Italian café ever had that winter. The Italians are a lively and passionate crowd. I'd have a bit of a chat with the boss-man and observe the people coming in and out the rest of the time. I think that there are probably a lot of people who've never been in one of these chip shops before, even if people with fairly steady work – the likes of myself – are in and out of them a lot. It's mainly the poor who frequent chip shops these days however and the shops all look the same. The walls are made of brown timber and wooden partitions divide the room into cubicles, and there's a table in every cubicle and seats. The smell of fish and potatoes fills the room and there's steam on the windows. There's nothing particularly beautiful about these places but the customers coming and going are worth observing. There are two types of people – the ones who bring the food home with them and the ones who eat it there and then. The first type go up to the counter and the manager serves up a load of fish and chips in a newspaper to them, then shakes salt and vinegar on it. Then they leave the shop again with that nice little parcel steaming under their arm. For many of the Dublin poor, this is their only food of the day. And I've seen crowds of people in these shops in the middle of the day and this is their main meal and all that they survive on. The second group of people often sit in for their meal, even if it's difficult enough for four people to sit together at a table. Their knees are all squashed together under the table and there's just about enough room for the plates and the food. Next, the box of salt and the vinegar bottle do the rounds from one person to the next and from table to table. Ragged-looking children stand outside the door all the while waiting for anything that might be left over. I learned a lot about the conditions that the Dublin poor endure that year. I found myself in shebeen houses a few times and they are places that can charge you twice the normal price for a bottle of beer. The last time I was in one, I found myself in a room where at least five or six people were living. A woman and two children were sleeping on a bed in the corner and a middle-aged woman also – the latter may have been the mother of the younger woman. Next thing, a young man arrived in who looked like he was the younger woman's husband. I gave out about the price of the beer that night and before I'd my bottle drunk even, two men were standing in the front door to stop me leaving. Undaunted however, I walked straight out past them and they made only a very lame attempt to stop me leaving. They were afraid that I'd be too strong for them, I'd say.

I never met as many people begging money on the streets as I did that year. Sometimes, I felt as if I was Harun Al-Rashid[2] dividing alms amongst the people. I came across every beggar under the sun – the sailor on crutches and the man who plays music with his hat cocked sideways and the long-bearded fellow playing the whistle and the man who barks like a dog (God save the mark!), the quiet, reserved man who sells shoelaces at pub doors, and the small blind man who's always on Daniel O'Connell Street in the morning and out in Dún Laoghaire come afternoon. None of these beggars was more fascinating to me however then the old, black-bearded fellow with eyes deep and dark and a pagan look about him whom I passed on the street each morning. He wore enough overcoats to cover Trinity College and they were all the colours of the weather, like the brow of a winter hill. Rain or shine, he always stood there in his own spot – it was all the same to him. I'd spotted him once or twice in passing and then I went over to him and put a penny into his old hat and asked him in the patter that was used in those days:

'Are you real or are you a demon? Can you feel pain or sorrow? Are you Bodach an Chóta Lachtna³ or Ceithearnach Caolriabhach Uí Dhónaill⁴ who returned to find the feast in full swing? Or are you the stranger that the Fianna⁵ used to meet on a dewy morning or the man who had a lucky escape from Argain Mhic Ancair na Long's⁶ crowd?'

He didn't understand me however. And I don't think he knew the answer to my question either. And me there thinking that I almost deserved the same reproach Colm Cille gave the man who asked questions he already knew the answers to!

I learned some new things about food that year also. I found out that I could buy enough milk and buttermilk for threepence as would do you. I got to know all the back-street cafés where the workers went and where you could buy bread and ham and tea for eight shillings. The people who went to these places were dirty looking and rough but anyone who says the poor have no dignity doesn't know them at all. And they're not ignorant either. I heard them debating many different issues and it amazed me how people as knowledgeable and intelligent as them were kept down and oppressed in the first place. I'd a habit of kicking off a debate or discussion and then keeping it going by throwing in my own tuppence-worth every now and then.

'There's hardly anyone working these days,' a man says one day.

'Maybe one out of every ten and the other nine living off that one man.'

'That reminds me,' I says, 'of a time when I left my hat in an office somewhere by accident and I had to write my name down on twenty forms before I could get it back again. If I'd left my trousers somewhere by mistake, there wouldn't be enough paper in Dublin for me to get them back again.'

'The people in power lack knowledge and understanding,' the man says.

'It's worse than that again,' I says. 'Too much knowledge and understanding is what that shower have.'

Unfortunately, I have neither time nor opportunity to recount the many conversations and debates I heard in different cafés and pubs back then or the discussions I had down by the quays with men who'd travelled the entire world; or the back-answers I gave guards or my insolence with shopkeepers and the thousand other ways I interacted with humanity in those days.

It really killed me whenever I was short of tobacco back then and I was so bad once or twice that I walked out the roads leading from the city in search of cigarette butts. Many people walk these roads and on a dry day you can collect a full basket of cigarette butts along them. One day, I even walked the full twelve miles from Dublin to Bray filling all my pockets on the way. This was a new form of sport the way I saw it, even if it was one that people hadn't engaged in professionally as of yet. When the heavy snow fell in the spring of 1933, I was giving an Irish-language class one day and my shoes were so old and wrecked that I'd to take them off and walk home barefoot. A woman came to me that that year looking for someone to teach her children. Her husband had been killed in Easter Week 1916 and she'd received a pension and such-and-such a sum of money for the education of her family. I made a deal with her and something magical blossomed from this also. I was teaching two children, one young lad aged fourteen and the other aged twelve; normally a girl of about sixteen would join us also so's I could give her a hand with her lessons. We normally sat in the back room, a run-down, old place with broken chairs and a miserable look about it. A pitiful, little coal fire was burning the first day I did the class but the next day it was a just a few papers in the grate and later again there was no fire at all. The youngest of the boys was like most lads his age: he was diligent enough about his work but he was never going to set the world on fire. You'd have taken note of the eldest lad however. He was gloomy and argumentative and unless he got his own way, you couldn't teach him anything. It was hard to make out whether he was very scattered in himself or whether he was just a young pup.

I was a week teaching there when the mother came into me one day with a crestfallen look and told me that her money hadn't arrived yet, that the civil servants were very slow at paying out and that she wanted me to wait another week for my wages. I gave her a week's grace. The following week she came to me with the same story.

'When Liam (this was her eldest son) makes enquiries with them,' she says, 'they ask him ridiculous little questions and try to catch him out on things with his replies. God help us, and the lad an orphan.'

'God might look out for Liam,' I says, 'but the civil servants won't. They're too petty-minded.'

I gave her another week's grace and the money eventually arrived. The day she paid me she was all chatty like before. She asked me questions about the children and said I should write up a report on how they were getting on. I wrote up the reference and praised them for their good points and left out their bad points.

'This'll be handy for me for the priest,' she says. 'He keeps a close eye on them. Do you know what they did on me there last year? I had them at school and they stole some books on me and sold them off, and ate whatever they made on them in some café or other and bought sweets with it. I found out about it and the president of the college wanted to send them to a reform school. But he let me off on the condition that they behaved themselves better from then on. I'm worried sick since – never knowing what they might get up to and that might land them in serious trouble. You'd swear that they'd committed some terrible crime the way they're so hard on them all the time.'

God sees it, I says to myself. These children had discovered too soon that this earthly life is based on stealing and living off the backs of others and now the world wants its pound of flesh back off them again. Anyone who says that this world is so honest and pure that children should be punished so severely for petty things, they are born liars – even if they were related to Saint Peter himself. Those poor small kids, they just weren't good enough at stealing. Woe to the man who strikes but leaves no mark.

I was nicer to the children after that and even when their homework was bad, I didn't get angry with them. To be honest, I've never had time for children who are good at school anyway. Most of them are just wasters.

The woman of the house had to take to the bed often. She suffered from shortness of breath and this was often so bad that an act of contrition was never far from her lips. One morning, just after I'd arrived, the girl came in and asked me for the loan of a shilling. In a baby voice nearly, she says:

'My mother is asking for a shilling.'

'Where is your mother?' I says.

'Asleep,' she says. 'She's looking for the loan of a shilling – for the week – to give to the bread man.'

My hand was in my pocket. All I had left was one shilling and three red pence. I fingered the coins and all the troubles of the world hurried through my mind. Normally I got my dinner from a caf somewhere and if I gave this shilling away, I'd have no dinner that day – and likely the following day either. But if I kept the money, the children might go hungry, and what did the term kinship mean realistically? Should I have behaved all hard-hearted towards these people seeing as they were cold and distant with me? Wasn't it in the Irishman's nature to be loyal to his own province, his own county, and his own way of life? But then, isn't every human being a member of the one family? If I came across a man who was drowning, would I wait to find out who he was before saving him? I took my hand from my pocket with the shilling in it. I'd have no dinner that day. But was going hungry for a while all that terrible really? But then again, how much would going hungry affect young children who forget it as quickly again once they get the next thing to eat? And isn't going without worse for the older person who expects life to provide its few basic comforts? The king without his crown or the poet without his music? Was I stupid to feel sorry for these kids just because their father died in 1916? What had Easter Week done for me?

I'd only been a child at the time myself and yet all they talked about in Dublin was – where were you in 1916?

A lion cub had arrived in Dublin the previous year but was quickly sent packing again, isn't that what they said? That they'd banished him to the corner, the same as Balor. And Balor hadn't been one bit happy about it either; there'd been an angry, wild grunt out of him and when the cub innocently approached him, he'd sent him flying across the room with one powerful swipe of his claw. 'Where were you in 1916?' he says. The old lion and his neighbours might have had English blood in them alright – but they'd been so long in this country as to become ipsis Hibernis Hiberniores. And wasn't it hard these days to tell the difference between the Gael and the foreigner anyway?

Were this family in as bad a way as they were making out? Weren't there thousands of families in Dublin that were far worse off than them? Had they asked lots of other people for the loan of a shilling too? Whatever other people thought and whether they gave them the shilling or not, they'd laugh at me and make out that I was a fool for being nice to them. I saw those devious little eyes of theirs mocking me. Wasn't I working cheaply enough for them as it was? Wasn't it the curse of the generous man that people never stopped asking him for things? They say that people have moments when their whole lives flash before them in a matter of seconds. And something similar happened to me in that very moment. The waves of my mind rolled in and the last one crashed to shore.

'I've no change at all,' I says.

I congratulated myself on my way home for being as strong-willed and firm as I'd been …

And when I got in the door, what was waiting for me but a letter with a cheque inside it. The widow died that night. When I went around to the house the following morning they were getting ready for the wake and there was no talk of classes. I drank that cheque. I wouldn't have only that I met an old lush who always brought me into the pub. Not that it was difficult to entice me in.

We went to a backstreet pub that was off the beaten track. Come ten o'clock, there were seven of us inside and they locked the doors and we went upstairs. By midnight, we were looking for a bit of music and the man of the house was kicking off the session with 'An Draighneán Donn'.[7] By two o'clock I was singing 'An Bhuinneáin Bhuí'[8] and so twist-ed-drunk that there was a fog between me and the green tablecloth. I had a sore head the following morning. The lodgings-woman brought in some slices of white bread and rotten butter, and an egg that was nine months old if it was a day, and a slice of bacon there that was like a bit of an old shoe – but I struggled to eat anything. All I had in my pocket was the one shilling and it was a wet morning outside.

I was inside suffering the hangover when a knock came on the door. I got up and opened it. A man stood there in rags so tattered and torn that you'd have sworn he'd been dragged through a ditch backwards for a week.

'For the love of God sir, but you wouldn't give me tuppence to get a bite of breakfast?'

I handed him my last shilling and turned to face the rotten butter and the old shoe leather and I soon had enough of them …

4

Oh, my mistake!

That winter in the lodgings I met some of the 'Nationalization' crowd or the Communists as some people call them. This wouldn't be worth mentioning really only that I got to know a strange man as a consequence. I went to a meeting of theirs one night when they had a lecture on the city poor. I heard what I was expecting to hear there: that the workers of today are like the slaves of long ago; that money and education are controlled by the one small group of people; that the wealth should be divided out so that everyone has a way to make a living; that every man has the same rights, and so on. Each of these small ideas was packaged within a whole heap of stirring and impressive words, the kind of terminology that everyone gathers the more they realize how the system really operates. I got up and said that

I'd learned a fair bit about poverty and the poor of Dublin in recent times and that I felt the speakers had got it all wrong.

'For one thing, I says, 'the slaves long ago were political prisoners or people who'd defied the legal system. Also, maybe they were treated more mercifully than if they'd been thrown into a frozen, grey-stone prison as happens with the likes of them today. But they aren't in the same situation as the workers nowadays. They became slaves by accident. But today's workers suffer under an unjust system; and anyone who's too dishonest or too corrupt or too weak somehow to stay within that system, they've abandoned the workers and live off the backs of the others, like maggots on a sheep. And that's not all either:

'I'd say that half of the people who work are reliant on the other half. And you could say that the human race today is divided into two types – those who earn the wealth – material or spiritual – or those who would do so if they had the opportunity, and those who live off the work of others. This latter group increases every hundred years that goes by. I think that the reason for this is that the workers who make the money and who produce the goods are in decline, that there aren't as many of them as there once was, and they aren't as effective as individuals as they were in the Middle Ages or even before that again. The statues and the pictures, the stories and poems and the tools and machines that they produced – the parasites and the maggots got control of them and they let on that they belong to them now. When push comes to shove, no one owns anything really except their own labour. And the biggest problem with the world today is that people think they can own something that they didn't make themselves. And once they've possession of this thing – whatever it is – they have to get rid of it again and exchange it with someone else. Also, the majority of people believe that if they benefit from this exchange, then they have the right to more clothes and more food and drink, and more respect and status. This failed form of exchange goes against the natural order however; if the natural system and balance of the stars was disturbed, then the world would explode, or burn up, or some other terrible thing would happen. For this reason, the human race will decline if we don't change our ways. And it's ridiculous to argue that the wealth should be divided out equally amongst all and sundry. It is the system of ownership of goods that has to be destroyed and that's something that you are all afraid of. You yourselves are just parasites who are unhappy with what you can skive off the system. If you were really serious about things you wouldn't be saying that it's the shopkeeper and the merchant class that control all the knowledge and wealth. All they have is a loan of the wealth and all they have is false knowledge. The man who has true knowledge isn't after what other people already possess. Many people today are looking for work but it isn't work that is badly needed but rather laziness or that which ignorant people refer to as laziness. Two thirds of the work undertaken nowadays goes to waste. A human being needs very little to get by on. And they can do a lot more for the intellectual and spiritual wealth of our society than they think. And this is where the real struggle exists; this is the element of humanity which every person is destroying for the other.

'Do you think that it's too difficult to produce enough potatoes and flour to serve the needs of the humanity? If it was, then people would be more focused on the issue of potatoes and flour. But this isn't so. That girl was burnt at the stake in France who said she'd received messages from heaven and Galileo was imprisoned for saying that the earth went around the sun.

'And that talk about everyone having the same rights and everyone being equal – that's all stupid talk. Actually, the way I see it, about forty-nine per cent of the population have an awareness and understanding of how society functions and fifty-one per cent don't. More than half of the human race are kept in a low and abandoned state – more so than any living person should have to endure. Anyone who thinks that the advantages provided by our system of exchange equate to being wealthy is lower than a brute because the brute has nothing but a brute's mentality in accordance with its nature.

'None of you should think,' I added, 'that you'll convince me the reason society is in such a state is because of the shopkeepers. It is human nature that's at the root of these problems and until we heal our own natures we're wasting our time talking about the struggle and class warfare.'

No one praised my words but no one criticized me either. I came too close to the truth. All they did was lower their heads with a frightened look as people do when they see someone make a fool of themselves. I've received the respect accorded to the fool a few times in my life and always when my words have meant the most. The greatest compliment that one man can pay another man's intellect is to deem him a fool when he is making the most sense. I went home and I was sitting smoking after breakfast the following morning when the woman of the house told me that someone was asking for me at the door and that he was the strangest-looking man she'd ever seen.

When I went down and saw this man I knew that she wasn't exaggerating. He wasn't a big man and yet his clothes were too small for him. Although he wasn't wizened looking, there was something completely misshapen about him and he was swarthy, the colour of a rodent. He was thin and you'd have sworn he had no strength in his limbs at all. His face was dark and sunken and so emaciated that you'd have sworn he hadn't eaten for a month. He was like someone who'd been kept inside on a dry loft for years so that he'd shrivelled away.

'Are you Mac Grianna?' he says

'I am,' I says.

'Dermot Lynch is my name,' he says. 'I heard you at the Communist meeting last night. You were the only one who said anything worthwhile there.'

He paused and handed me a letter and I looked at him in amazement. Surely, this fellow is after coming from Russia and his letter is instructing me to assume leadership of the western side of Europe. To tell you the truth, I got a bit of a fright. I looked at him again but he didn't utter a word.

'Come in for a minute,' I says and opened the letter. His handwriting was unusual. It was large and distinct, like a child's – a child with the mentality of someone much older. A glance at the letter told me that it was neither an order nor a communication but rather a series of deeply thought-out yet incomprehensible views on life and the world. 'People's good manners and pious talk are just a pretence' was how it began. 'Whenever someone thinks that they are really virtuous, they are blind to their own faults in reality. No one can be virtuous without constant vigilance and by mortifying themselves against every sort of pleasure. The man who is rich thinks that mortification has no function for him. The married man thinks that he is free of lust. Countries make war on each other when their riches and luxuries overwhelm them, etc.'

'You wrote this yourself?' I says, looking up from the letter.

'I did,' he says.

'A lot of deep thought has gone into this,' I says. 'But, tell me this. What did you think of that meeting last night?'

'They're all useless,' he says.

It was very difficult to make conversation with him. I gave it another go.

'The first thing Ireland needs, is to learn the Irish language again. Beginning this project is two thirds of the battle.'

'I don't think,' he says, 'that Irish is a learned language.'

'Oh, but you're wrong there,' I says. 'We've the oldest literature in Europe, Roman and Greek literature excepted.'

'There are only two genders in the Irish language,' he says, 'feminine and masculine. That's a bad sign of any language.'

'I never looked at it that way. There was definitely another gender in Old Irish. Maybe there's still a necessity for it,' I says, looking him up and down.

'It's bad if a language has only masculine and feminine,' he repeated. I noticed that there was nothing humble about his attitude and when he spoke in an intellectual way he never developed his ideas further. In fact, every word he uttered was slow and long drawn-out, as if he'd struggled to come up with it there and then.

He wasn't long inside the door when he handed me another letter. I read it and understood from him then that he preferred to communicate through letters. I asked him to come around any time he wanted. He called around the following week and he had another letter with him. He kept calling around for a long time and most of his communication was through this medium of letters. He rarely spoke but he did tell me once that he was from County Limerick originally and that he'd been left a big inheritance so that he had seventeen and six of a weekly allowance and that he was trying to live off this. He had a room in one of the back streets.

He was someone that you couldn't make free with. And all I ever got to know of him was when I opened the door every now and then to find him standing there when I was least expecting it – like a hungry bird in the depths of winter.

I passed him three or four times on the city streets making that slow, lumbering way of his along through the living tide of humanity. The last time I saw him, he was growing a beard. The beard was black and about an inch and a half long and if he looked strange before, he was stranger looking still with the beard. He never let on to recognize me on the street and I often wondered whether he had many other people like me that he called into on those strange visits of his. I'm afraid that he hadn't. He'd only have been interested in people who were deep thinkers. Most people wouldn't have made conversation with him – no more than a black crow would keep company with a red one. I don't know how he passed his days unless it was working on these letters and short, silent essays of his. I don't know whether he grew the beard in the absence of a razor or whether it was a visible sign of some kind of internal spiritual growth he'd achieved. I don't know what happened to him either after the last time I saw him moving as a stranger amongst the crowd. If you've ever walked through a gallery of paintings you've probably noticed a painting here and there that grabbed your attention. You've stood momentarily in front of that painting and after a while you've walked away and forgotten about it again. You neither took to it nor did you reject it. That's how it was between me and Dermot Lynch also.

5

My new lodgings was close to the sea and I had plenty of opportunities to walk along the shore. I was brought up near the sea and have always loved walking on the beach. My home-place was more beautiful than most but every shore has its own character. This was the first time that I found myself cooking for myself and although I had no practice at it, I didn't do too badly, and it never took up too much time either. I usually ate two big meals a day and was free to do my own thing the rest of the time.

It was summer and I spent a lot of time outdoors sun-bathing. In fact, I was out in the sun so much that summer the heat went right into my bones. I suffered a strange illness that year also. For three days, I felt incredibly down and depressed. It was the worst thing I've ever experienced and I was totally exhausted and had no energy whatsoever. I had no inclination to go outdoors either even if the weather was so beautiful that most people were outside. As far as I could tell I hadn't damaged my health or brought this illness on myself in any way. And I wasn't physically sick with it either. Sometimes I thought that maybe I'd overdone it and spent too much time out under the sun.

Tom Kerrigan called around to me fairly often in those days. He'd call into me early in the morning or late at night. One morning I was getting my breakfast ready when he arrived in.

'There's a man out here,' he says, 'and if you don't mind, I'd like you to give him some breakfast. I met this poor fellow and he was in such a bad way that he was about to cut his own throat. He slept outside last night.'

'Go out and tell him to come in,' I says.

He arrived in a minute later, with a tall, thin man.

'This is MacNaughton.'

'Good morning MacNaughton,' I says. 'Sit down.'

'He slept outside last night,' Tom said, 'and himself and I are going to put our heads together and see what's the best thing for him to do.'

'A bite of breakfast won't do him any harm anyway,' I says, getting up and putting the kettle on. At the same time I gave the man a quick glance and noticed that his clothes were fairly nice, even if they were a bit old and worn. He didn't look like someone who'd slept outside the previous night.

'Where did you sleep?' I asked.

'Down by the canal bank' he said.

'Sleeping outdoors isn't good for you, even if it is summer. Have you been homeless for long?'

'Five or six months. I was stupid and got a small loan from the bank that I couldn't pay back.'

'It doesn't matter a damn about that, between ourselves,' I says.

'You'd be a long time borrowing from the bank before you'd get anywhere near the amount of money the bank itself has taken on loan from others.'

'Do you think that the Russians have it right?' he says.

'I think that they have it right in some ways,' I says, 'but I don't think that they're right about everything.'

'I don't think that they have it right,' he says. 'I don't think you can deny God.'

'You can't,' I says, 'but the majority of the world denies Him nowadays and most of them still let on they believe in something. Given the way they attack false religions, it's not surprising at all that true religion gets the odd bashing also. As the old saying goes: "It's the innocent who always suffer."'

'People's spiritual beliefs enrich their minds,' he says. 'You can't understand spirituality without studying the human mind. One part of the mind is spiritual and that's God's part. The other part is rough, hard, intellectual, and that's the devil's part.'

On hearing this, I threw my head back and shut both my eyes – a habit I have when the mind is stimulated. It was a long time since I'd heard talk as powerful as this. Over the years, I've often asked myself how come there are fools who have insight and intelligent men who appear unable to see to the heart of things at all.

'God overcame the devil,' I says, 'and sent him to hell. But it's rare that the spirit overcomes the mind in human beings. I'd say you've probably heard this one before:

> God did all good with his word
> But original sin did the damage
> It is our hope in times of difficulty
> that God will prevail
> and yet the devil still casts a spell.

This is what's troubling us all in this era – that we can see quite clearly that the devil is present and knows his business. But your breakfast is ready now and I'm sure that it was from God that we got a good appetite. Sit yourself down there.'

He ate plenty but it didn't fill him at all.

'I don't know what's the best thing for him to do tonight?' says Thomas.

'I don't know,' I says. 'I'm afraid that I can't help much anyway. I'm a writer and many's the rainy day I've seen.'

'I was thinking that you were a writer alright,' he says, 'when I saw all the paper lying around. I've often thought of writing something myself.'

'If you've an idea for a story you should begin on it.'

'I do,' he says. 'I have a story, a true story and it would be worth writing, I think. It is good proof that human beings have a soul and that two souls can be in contact with one another, even if separated by hundreds of miles, and even if one person is dead and buried beneath the earth. Two people in our place were promised to one another. The man was a captain in the army. A war began and he had to go away to fight and leave the girl by herself. He wrote home to her regularly for a year or so and then the news came that he'd been killed. Everyone believed that he was dead except for this girl. She refused to believe it and said that she was sure he would return someday from the war. The pair of them had a path they always followed out through the glen when they went for walks. The girl would go out alone for walks nearly every day. Two years went by and there was no word of the captain. One afternoon the girl went out for a walk in the glen when something gave her a terrible fright, the same as if a bullet had whistled past her ear. She felt weak and collapsed and had to be brought home. She was bedridden permanently after that. Everyone thought that she'd had some kind of a mental breakdown because she was always saying that the captain would return one day to the glen and she was afraid that she wouldn't be around when he appeared. The doctor said that she had a weak heart and that she wouldn't live very long. But she really wanted to stay alive until the captain returned. She said that when she'd gone out walking that day she was certain that the young man had appeared and stood next to her, although she couldn't see him or hear him. Eventually, she passed away. Her corpse was still laid out in the house when a man was seen standing at the foot of the tree where she'd collapsed that day. It was the captain.'

'You have the bones of a good story there,' I says. 'And it would be easy for you to write it up one day. The most difficult thing these days is just to survive at all. Are you long sleeping outdoors?'

'The woman in charge of the lodgings kicked me out yesterday morning,' he says. 'I haven't a penny to my name and I've nowhere to go either.'

'Unfortunately I don't have much money,' I says, 'all I have is this little room here and this bed. You can come in here tomorrow morning and get your breakfast. That's all the help I can give you. There are writers around who have money though.'

'Do you know such-and-such a person?' he says, naming a certain writer who lived close by.

'I do,' I says, 'and maybe he'd help you.'

The names of five or six different writers came up in conversation then. We continued chatting until he felt that it was time for him to leave.

'How did you first meet him?' I says to Tom when he was gone.

'I met him up in H—Park,' he says. 'He asked me for a cigarette first. Then he started chatting to me and told me that he would have done himself in only that I'd come along. I gave him two shillings.'

'As long as there's a sun in the sky, the generous man won't see hell,' I says, 'but I don't think for a minute that he had any intention of killing himself. Not that it matters – he's still one of the strangest people I've met in a long time. And you'd have no business making conversation about the weather with him. I hope he comes back again tomorrow morning.'

I didn't need to wait until the following day however. That afternoon I was told that there was a man outside looking for me. I went down and found MacNaughton standing at the door.

'I was thinking afterwards about writing that story,' he says. 'I got my hands on some paper but I've nowhere to write it. I was wondering whether you might be able to let me in here for a while.'

'I'm just going out,' I says, 'and it wouldn't be easy for me to let you in once I'm gone. Come here tomorrow and you can have your breakfast and don't forget that story in the meantime. We'll get there.'

The following morning Tom was in early and MacNaughton wasn't long behind him.

'I hope you had a good bed last night?' I says.

'I did,' he says. 'I ran into a friend of mine.'

'It's not easy for the poor man to have a friend these days,' I says. 'I never had any friends except people who were nearly as poor as myself. And it's amazing how many people are in dire straits. I never understood this properly until I found myself down on my luck. I see a raggedy-looking young lad up there at the corner every day working a machine that's like a churn, twisting the handle of it and churning out music. No one listens to him and no one even looks at him when they are passing. I don't know how he survives at all. Mind you, the likes of him are usually a lot richer than you think.'

'It'd be worth someone's while getting their hands on one of those music-making devices,' says Tom 'and going around the country with it.'

'I was thinking the same thing myself,' I says. 'There's no musical instrument made yet that I could ever make a fist of – but I'd be sure to see a bit of the world standing there on the side of the road and all I'd have to do is keep twisting my hand around and around. It'd be a poetic existence.'

I was thinking to myself of forming a group between the three of us and was hoping to plant the seed in MacNaughton's mind by suggesting something a bit crazy and unusual. But he didn't get it or have much of a sense of humour either. He didn't react at all and I changed the subject.

'Whoever's poor is always in a serious bind and no one in Ireland has any sympathy for them – unless they're a drunk or they die young. I don't understand why this is?'

This line of conversation didn't seem to get him going either however. I've often run into people who have a surface understanding of the truth but when you dig down deeper to the heart of it, I find myself on my own.

'The country is in a bad way,' I says. 'We've forgotten how to till the land and the English didn't let us buy any machines either. There's no work in this country except politics.'

'I don't like politics,' says MacNaughton. 'Politics is just a load of wind.'

'Still and all, the odd thing comes out of it,' I says. We made some stilted conversation like this but MacNaughton wasn't as interested in conversation as he'd been the day before. He wasn't long leaving again this time.

'We won't see him again,' I says to Tom. But I was wrong. He was back again a few hours later.

'I have that music-machine for you,' he said.

'God, I wasn't expecting that,' I replied.

'I was talking to the lad who's always working it. I can get one of them for you for five or six shillings. If you give me six shillings right now, I'm fairly sure I can get it for you.'

'Don't mind it,' I said. 'I was only messing anyway.'

'Oh,' he says. 'I thought you were serious.'

I thought it'd be hard to get rid of him this time but it wasn't. He turned on his heel and was gone. I spotted your man with the music-churn up at the corner, waiting for him.

'Did you ever hear tell of what the scholars call the food chain?' I says to Tom the following day. 'Out in the wild, when a lion kills a cow, it eats some of it and leaves the rest behind. There's another wild animal again waiting for the lion to leave so as to get the leftovers. And another wild animal again, waiting on the leftovers left behind by the second animal. It's the same with the human race. There's hardly anyone these days who's not living off someone else. MacNaughton asked you for a cigarette and in that way, he got to know me, and then he brought the music-box man in on top of me. The chain was getting longer every day and it'd be as long as the Shannon by now only that I nipped it in the bud and cut us loose.'

'Do you think he wasn't telling us the truth?' says Tom.

'I think he was in a bad way alright, but I'm sure that he's been that way for years. He would have been more honest in my eyes if he hadn't tried to flog that music-box thing on me. I had enough of him then. But I really liked the tricks he got up to. When he met you he'd nothing amazing to say for himself. Any beggar could have told you that he'd slept outside and that he was thinking of doing himself in. But when he came and talked to me, he did it in a very clever way. Whether it was a guess on his part, to bring the conversation around to religion and Russia, it was a good one – but if he did it deliberately, then it was a very cute move altogether because these are questions that I'm often reflecting on during the winter months. Then, when he told us about the story he had, and I urged him to write it down, he thought he was away with it. I'm a bit worried now that I didn't let him keep going – to see what he'd get up to next.'

'What do you think he was really up to?' says Tom.

'I saw him looking out the window and down the length of the garden there,' I says. 'But I don't know if he was up to something or not. Maybe he was hoping I'd left some money lying around.'

'I heard tell of a man named MacNaughton who was a well-known tramp over in Argentina,' says Tom. 'Maybe he's the same man.'

'Stranger things have happened,' I says.

6

The following week I met a man who was high up in the IRA. I'd got to know him five or six years earlier, as it happens. He was always asking me to join up but there was something in me that told me not to give in to him. This wasn't my own road either. Something got into me this particular day however and I decided to lead him on a bit. He came out of a shop where his car was parked outside on the road.

'Why don't you organize some kind of an action?' I says. 'The way things are going, people are beginning to forget that Ireland ever wanted a Republic. The Communist rabble allowed their place to be burnt down. But when your neighbour burns your house down, there's only one response to that, and that's to burn his place down too. Shur, that crowd aren't really serious about things at all.'

'Listen my friend,' he says. 'If you've got truth on your side, you can't hide behind a bush with it. They're only letting on that they're Communists and Irishmen and Catholics all in one.'

'I can't see why they can't be all three things,' I says. 'In my opinion, they're none of them really.'

'Hang on,' he says. 'I've a car outside. Do you want to come with me for the spin?'

'Where are you headed?' I says.

'Right around Ireland,' he says.

'I'll go out with you the whole way,' I says.

He was happy. We sat in and I could tell that he was very proud of the car. He drove very slowly and carefully and I could tell what he was thinking – someone like me should be proud just to be sitting in a car the likes of his. But I always judge someone for themselves and not by what they own. That's why I put my feet up on tables in cafés and leave a cloud of cigarette smoke behind me in shops and offices. We went out onto the main road in the direction of Meath, chatting all the while.

'Pearse did great things,' I says. 'There's no one in Ireland that wasn't heartened by what was achieved in 1916. But it did a lot of damage too. I remember walking through Dublin city centre one day and spotting two guards, looking very angry. A dishevelled, ragged-looking woman was caught between the pair of them, pissed as a coot, and she bawling at the top of her voice:

> Mid cannon's roar and rifle's peal,
> We'll chant a Soldier's Song.

You're well able to take credit for other people's work, I thought to myself.'

I thought he'd just laugh at this but he took what I said to heart instead.

'If there are people in this world who've no manners, there's nothing we can do about it,' he says. 'There were always bad eggs amongst us, people who were weak, people who were easily bought.'

'Well, you can't really say that that drunken woman was easy bought,' I says, 'but there you go ... Do you not think that maybe we're not really worth that much anyway when it comes down to it?'

'I have my price the same as the next man, he says, 'and I'm worth more than most.'

'My price is so high that no one could ever buy me,' I says. 'I don't think politics could buy me. Although, maybe it could, if I knew what your crowd were thinking of doing if you were elected.'

He kicked off and went into great detail describing what I'd heard and read a hundred times before – until I stopped him, that is.

'That's enough, please,' I says. 'That's all very well and fine but will you smash up the telephones and burn all the forms?'

'Oh, for sure, I'd be really worried if there was as much time wasted as there is on many things these days.'

'You're not too bad at all really,' I says. 'And night's drawing in and we're heading west on a journey that not everyone makes. I think Uisneach[1] is close by and do you see that old castle covered in grass and bushes? Whoever let it get overgrown with grass like that knows very little of their own history, isn't it true for me?'

'All I can see wrong with it is that the place is no good for grass or grazing even,' he says. 'An old ruin lying there for years under the wet and rain.'

'Don't say that,' I says. 'There was a time once when that place was the heart of humanity and civilization in this area, and even if its day is gone, don't think for a minute that it didn't leave its mark on history. The people who built that castle are in the same class as the people who built Saint Peter's in Rome and created great art and poetry, and who explored the entire world. The Gaels say that two art-forms are dying – poetry and craftsmanship. I think that there's a good deal else dying with them in the present era.'

We continued on our way, debating this and that, as dusk fell in the trees on both sides of the road. We passed gates and houses nestled in clumps of trees. Lights appeared on both sides of us like stars as we passed through small villages, quiet and peaceful, along the way. Eventually, when it was nearly dark, your man stopped the car.

A tall, slow-moving man dressed in black stood beneath the trees like a ghost. He greeted us and got into the back of the car. We left the main road then and the ghost gave us directions as we passed through a series of different crossroads.

'Are you busy these days Seán?' says the driver.

'Nothing doing for a while now,' said the ghost, 'but a new man came to the barracks recently. It won't be long before he comes sniffing around, I'd say.'

After we'd gone three or four miles, the car pulled in at a gate and the ghost disappeared.

'We're going in here,' says the boss – we'll call him Liam Cassidy.

Liam was a city man. I could tell this as we went up the avenue to the house because although the path was fairly smooth he was like a blind man tip-toeing on the gravel. A fellow in his thirties seemed to be looking after the house. The kitchen had an open fire of the old style large enough for a horse to stand in and hobs on either side to warm yourself. He had a fire made of twigs and branches down. This wasn't coal or turf country. The man made some food for us – whether he wanted to or not.

There was no mention of war or people's rights and the talk wasn't particularly interesting – more like a chat between two men who know each other well. I could tell from the conversation that this man was a commander and the horror and the poetry was kept hidden from anyone lower down the food chain – the likes of me. This is the way of the world, I says to myself. Nothing much happened there and eventually we left the house and crossed the Shannon and reached Galway sometime between dusk and time for sleep. We called into another man then but I couldn't say that anything incredible happened there either.

We stayed that night in a hotel and travelled cross-country the following day until we reached a certain town directly south of Galway city. It was fair day and sturdy, sharp-eyed men stood on the road buying and selling live-stock. We went into a house halfway down the street and waited there a half an hour or so for someone to call. Then who arrived in but the local priest. He was a young, handsome man and very welcoming. We sat down and discussed how the fighting had gone in 1922 and what should have been done better as regards tactics and strategy so on. We were there almost an hour when the man arrived that Cassidy was waiting to meet. He was a young, black-haired lad and couldn't stop talking. He seemed really stressed.

'No one's listening to me these days except for the ones who are half-mad,' he says, 'and the CID² haven't left us alone for three days. And I wouldn't mind that if it wasn't that my family are already at their wit's end and ready to throw me out of the house because of the stress of it. I can't stick it much longer.'

The priest spoke to him and tried to calm him down and talk sense into him and so did Cassidy, and then I tried too – and believe me, it took a good while. We spent the rest of the afternoon talking and eventually Cassidy handed the lad a letter and sent him on his way.

'Now,' he says. 'I've to go out the country as it'll be night soon. If they're ahead on the road, looking out for us, at least we have each other for company. You're not afraid, are you?'

'No, not at all,' I says. 'I can understand you being anxious as you've certain responsibilities that you've to fulfil on the way. But I couldn't care less where the sun rises on me. I'm not so reliant on other people that I'd be bothered by them one way or another – whether they're a help or a hindrance, it makes no difference to me,' I says.

'What's that up ahead?' he says after we were just a few minutes on the road.

'That's them,' I says, 'but if we don't drive right through them, then this whole trip will have been a waste of time.'

We drove right through the checkpoint and one man got a belt of the car bumper that sent him flying head-first onto the ground. The guards didn't fire on us despite this however. A half an hour later I checked behind us to see were we being followed.

'There's a car following us,' I says.

'That's no surprise at all,' says Liam. 'If they're not waiting for us up ahead – they'd have to be behind us.'

'You're turning into the right witty buck now, aren't you?' I says. 'You're sharper than your usual type for sure, I've noticed that. It's amazing how danger enhances the mind.'

The car behind us continued to follow us until night fell, it was pitch-dark and we'd passed into County Mayo. I looked behind us again and noticed that we were now further away from them than we'd been earlier.

'We're losing them,' I says.

'You're right,' says Cassidy turning round. 'They've stopped.'

'You're right,' I says, 'maybe it was just a few women out for a spin with their pet dogs.'

We reached Westport that night and stayed in a man's house there and delivered a letter to him. The following day as we approached Sligo I brought up the letters.

'It's amazing,' I says, 'that we've covered so many miles by car for the sake of a few letters. I'm a bit dubious about these letters – how important are they really?'

'Well, we have to give them something,' he says.

'If guns were as plentiful as letters, this trip might be worth it.'

'Do think that guns would do the job?' he says.

'Even one gun itself would do fair damage,' I says. 'If we had one now we could fire off a few bursts in Mullingar and then in Athlone, and then in Ballinasloe and in Galway city and so on.'

'It would only take them a few hours to trace the car with the gun though.'

'My good man,' I says, 'that's not how it'd go at all. The minute they heard the shots in Mullingar, everyone would be thinking how they could manipulate the situation to their own advantage. They'd try and surround the place with a square mile of defences. And the same in all the other towns. They'd have the army nearby as back-up and then you'd have the rest of the country free for yourselves to get up to whatever you wanted.'

'You're too hard on the people,' he says.

'Ah, I'm not really. Shur, I'm as big a rogue as anyone when it comes down to it, even if I do have the occasional scruple of conscience from time to time.'

We travelled on to Sligo to a place where a young lad was waiting for us in an old room that had once been a shop. Everything was covered in dust and dirt and there were leaflets lying around as if printing had been done there at one stage also. But one look at the boy's face told you that nothing much had happened there for a long time. He was a small, pale, young lad and you couldn't read anything from his face other than that he had no importance within the Movement.

'Have you any good tips for the races Seán?' Liam says and the conversation turned to horse racing.

'I thought the horses went out of fashion during the war?' I said later as we sat in a hotel eating dinner. 'I thought the crash of hooves and the thrill of the chase, and the flash of the spurs that decorated the battlefields of old disappeared years ago.'

'The only thing that the horses are useful for now,' Liam says, 'is racing. Lots of people will bet on them and you'll have a racecourse full of people gathered together and eager to see which horse gets its nose out that inch or two in front of the next one.'

'You're not a big horse racing fan, are you?' I says.

'No, I'm not,' he says, 'but I'm a big fan of Seán's.'

We left Sligo late that afternoon and travelled east in the direction of Dublin. The night was peaceful. The moon rose as we as we climbed the brow of a mountain and the clouds were scudding across the backs of the hills.

'That's Cornaslieve Pass,' says Liam.

We went through Boyle as far as Longford and from there towards Cavan and it was very late by the time we reached Cavan. We were sitting in a hotel in Cavan town when we heard a powerful roar from somewhere outside.

'That's a sick cow calving, I'd say,' Liam says in a knowledgeable tone of voice.

'Each to their own opinion,' I says, 'but no cow ever made a sound like that before and I don't remember a sick cow ever bellowing loudly like that either. The animal that made that roar can only be found in one place and that's in Dublin.'

'In Dublin?'

'Yes, that's the roar of a lion!'

The girl came around a short while later and we enquired about the lion. She said that there was a circus in town and that they were camped in the field opposite us.

'Wasn't he the lucky one who got the drop of the bees-tings!' I says and she gave me a stare.

'We thought it was a sick cow,' I says, and Liam gave me a look that was worse than the belt of a stick.

The next day we were on our way again and nothing major happened until we were back in Dublin. I returned to my lodgings like the man who has just returned from his holidays. The city seemed lifeless and dead to me and I paced up and down the floor of my room until midnight. I'd gone halfway around the roads of Ireland and yet my mind felt confined and hemmed in. I felt imprisoned. I was trapped in that small, strange room once more – a place that was neither here nor there. I was depressed falling asleep that night and yet I also sensed that something unusual would happen to me before too long.

7

Come the following morning, I was in such a hurry to escape that room and get outside into the fresh air that I could tell I was coming down with a bout of depression. Whenever I start feeling down like this, I make a break for the country and the wild loneliness of the bogs and hills. I've always experienced these moods and impulses – the feeling of the 'blues' – and poetry often emerges from them. The loneliness of the country is similar to the drunkenness of poetry. They are like the gifts that Moses brought to Mount Sinai and that John the Baptist brought across the Jordan with him. Your perception expands out in the desolation of the countryside – the vision that is mind and soul – and despite how clever people are today, they still don't comprehend this. But if the human race ever evolves properly one day they will surround every town and city with great lonely gardens, many miles in size.

I left the city and went out to the place where the fittest men go swimming – at the Forty Foot. But it was too crowded out there and so I circled the shoreline for a mile or so – out to the strand at Dalkey, where I found myself completely alone. I walked out to the edge of a cliff there and stretched out on a rock, sunning myself. The day was so beautiful it would have broken your heart, it was so magnificent that you never wanted it to end – the sun so bright and the air so sweet and pure. The smell of the sea and the movement of the tide gave me huge strength and I felt a wildness in me. The sea always gives me incredible energy and strength, particularly from the psychological point of view. I've often thought if I was living by the sea and had the notion to write a book, I'd write a work that would blow most people's minds.

But I had no inclination of writing anything that day at all, I was too restless. Walking and other things were on my mind. Since I'd begun forging my own road, I'd stopped writing and now I was questioning myself as to whether I could live both lives simultaneously – the wandering life and the artistic life of the mind. Could a man sit by the edge of the sea and appreciate the joy and beauty of the horizon far away – and yet also take to his boat and enjoy the true purity of air and sky on that same horizon? This internal struggle disturbed me and I had to get up and follow the thin tidal streams down by the shore, as they twisted and turned on the courses laid out for them. I wandered around aimlessly until darkness fell and I felt tired again and went home.

I went out to Howth the second day and to Glenasmole on the third – but I couldn't relax in either place. Then I noticed that all I had left in the world was eighteenpence and I no longer went in search of solitude anymore after that. Tom Kerrigan called into me one day.

'Tom,' I says, 'all I've left in this world is eighteenpence and it's a long-held custom of mine that when I reach my last few shillings, I go out and drink them. And good luck always follows from this. That's my latest plan. Come on out with me for the crack.'

'I'm off the drink,' he says.

'No matter, you can have apple juice or something. Let's go!'

We bought beer and apple juice and made the drinks last as long as we could and I went home that night, happy as a piper. The following morning, I had enough food in for breakfast and then I spent the day hanging around St Stephen's Green. There's no one in Dublin that hasn't passed through St Stephen's Green but only a few people have taken note of anything other than the trees and the lake and George the Second on the back of his horse. But the person who observes life carefully will see a lot in St Stephen's Green if they really want to. The place is thick with foliage and grass and these are of great value to anyone that feels life grinding them down. Sitting on the bench there, I reflected on what people call the noise and chaos beyond those park gates – the battle that is life!

No, by my soul, that's not it, I says to myself – it's really the flight from hunger. There's not one man in every hundred thousand scrabbling around in this city today that has real guts. They're all running away from something. The person with real heart who's willing to face the menace of the world head-on is probably resting inside here in this park at this very moment. This thought gave me strength and did me instead of my dinner. A man sat close by and you could tell by his clothes that he was right in the thick of it, right at the heart of the battle. He had a notebook out and if he'd been reading Plato he couldn't have been deeper in concentration. Although he was just five or six feet away from me, I could see that the book he had out was a timetable for the races. A couple of other people sat slightly further on from this man talking very loudly.

'Do you see that man?' one of them says, pointing their finger in the direction of a tall stooped man in rags who was walking around talking to himself.

'That man had 100,000 pounds once and he lost the lot.'

I got up and walked around the park and I wasn't long gone when I heard a voice behind me:

'Is it yourself there?'

This man was from Scotland and he'd spent some of his life in Australia and he'd also fought in the Great War of 1914. He'd been on a ship that had been sunk and he'd been left for dead for a few days afterwards. His family were Irish originally. I'd met him in a lodging house a long time before and we were friendly in a way that people who are afraid to talk to strangers don't understand. He was very interested in Irish politics and we chatted about this for a while. He left again and I walked around the park and began to feel hungry once more. Finally, I left the Green altogether and walked through the city streets. Two or three beggars waylaid me but

I had to shake my head and walk on. I wasn't in a position to help anyone out. Now and again, I came across people I knew. When I was doing well, they'd have been straight over to me and ready to shake my hand, and I could have relied on the majority of them. But now, even if I didn't look that down-and-out, I could have sworn that they knew I hadn't eaten anything since morning and they were quick to pass me by on the other side of the road. At least I had the small satisfaction now that boring people steered clear of me – that was something anyway.

After I'd walked around like this for nearly two hours, I came across a large building with the name Salvation Army written in big letters above it. Everything I'd ever heard about this group came to mind. It mightn't be a bad idea for me to try them, I thought, seeing as I was down on my luck. One of the Army's soldiers came out to me from a kind of the cubicle at the back and he wanted to put me on the list of beggars. I wanted to see their leader first, I told him, and I got my way. I said to their leader that I was thinking of joining their army and I said all the right things about how interested I was in their way of life – until he accepted me. I left their place again with my belly full, a few pence in my pocket, and a batch of War Cries under my arm. I didn't sell too many of these newspapers however. I showed them to many people, a Catholic bishop amongst them. The Mayor of Dublin bought one from me and I sold one to a German who was on holidays and who had no English at all, and another to a man who was drunk. Tom Kerrigan bought two of them from me and I kept three for myself. I returned to the Army and they told me that I'd done really well.

I was sorted for the week and when Sunday came around, I joined a group who went out sermonizing on the streets. We stood down by the banks of the Liffey where the buses come in. I don't know whether anyone recognized me that day seeing as half the world passes that way. And it's always when you're in a crowded place and when you least expect it that someone will spot you. No one bothered listening to us other than a half-a-dozen poor and raggedy-looking men leaning against the quay walls there. Does the gospel hold such little interest in today's world, I asked myself. We began singing one of the army's hymns, one that I didn't know myself. I'm not a singer – that's for sure. Hardly anyone has ever heard me try and sing – other than a girl who was as good a singer as anyone in Dublin and who told me once that I had an ear for music. I'd often thought that if I tried it and learned how to project my voice, I might have made a singer – given that every singer has their own style, the same as every writer. It's only stupid for someone to tell me that you'd have to have the eight notes for a start. That's just the small stuff of music. It's the big things that matter: feeling and purity of voice, and a sense of drama – aspects that are hidden to the majority of singers but which come to me fairly naturally.

Anyway I didn't have the guts to join in the Army's hymn even if I was ashamed to remain silent too. I tried to think of what song I knew best. I thought back to my early child-hood until I remembered it and then struck up with a voice brimming with hope:

Beir scéala uaim siar chun na Rosann
Ionsar an Dálach arb ainm dó Aodh,

Gur éalaigh an Chrúbach as Toraigh
'S go ndeachaigh sí anon ar an ghaoth;
Ní raibh ann ach a cnámha 's a craiceann
'S nach láidir mar chuaigh sí chun scaoil,
Gan coite bád ina haice
A bhéarfadh go seascair í i dtír?

Bring news from me back to the Rosses
To the man of the Daly's by the name of Hugh
That An Chrúbach has escaped from Tory
And has gone over on the wind;
She was just skin and bone
But did she not escape with great strength
With neither skiff nor boat beside her
Which would bring her calmly ashore?

If the others noticed me, they didn't let on anything even if I noticed the workers by the wall getting restless. The curiosity of Dublin workers is always pricked whenever they hear Irish – and they were probably thinking that this Army finally had someone who could spread the gospel in the language of Saints Bríd and Colm Cille. They looked me up and down and whispered to one another in a way that was deadly serious. Maybe they thought that it was time for the Church to excommunicate me officially. We continued with our singing all the same:

Onward Christian soldiers,
Marching us [sic] to war!

and I sang:

75

A Dhónaill, nach cuimhin leat le n-aithris
Mar tugadh an Ghlas Ghaibhleanna Mhór
Go Toraigh ar lorg a rubaill
Agus tháinig sí ar ais go tír
Oh Dónall, don't you remember
The tale of An Glas Ghaibhleann Mhór[1]
How she came to Tory in search of her own tail
And returned to the mainland once more?

This song gave me such encouragement that I felt like launching into a sermon in Irish right then but it wasn't my turn to give the sermon till the next day. Come the following day, I felt guilty about the whole thing however. It wasn't in my make-up or nature to join the harvest with the Salvation Army, no matter how well-intentioned they were. I thought back to that day long ago when the Salvation Army had visited my native village for the first time.

I believe that Rannafast is the most Gaelic village in Ireland. It is situated between two quiet and peaceful inlets in the part of Ireland that is furthest away from London and Normandy. And there's no part of Rannafast more isolated from the outside world than An Bháinseach. It is there that young people gather on a Sunday afternoon in spring and summer when the tide is full and as smooth as glass – and Béal na Trá Báine can be seen over to the west and Carraig na Spáinneach, where an Armada ship lies hidden beneath a deep mound of sand.

And An Bháinseach is where the Salvation Army came ashore that time. They blew their foreign trumpets and played their strange music, and the Milesian Tribe busy working the fields, saving hay, and cutting corn and giving a thousand thanks to God for the fine weather. But the priest we had at the time happened to be going around the village that day and he was a unique character, so much so that they still tell stories about him. He was proud and he was bitter and he was witty too; and even if there was a lot of Colm Cille about him, there was much more of Conán Maol in him. And the minute he spotted the Salvation Army, he knew he had trouble on his hands. There was a big stack of turf on An Bháinseach at the time that had been brought down to the shore to burn kelp in a kiln there. The priest set himself up behind the load of turf there and attacked the Army people, throwing turf in their direction. He really went for them, firing sod after sod in their direction until he forced them to run away – I'm not sure now whether it was out by Bealach Gaoithe way or up by Bearnas Éamainn Bhrádaigh they escaped but such a scattering of the British wasn't seen since Cornaslieve Day.

I was recalling all of this as I went down to the Salvation Army Hall the following morning. I knew that I wasn't a suitable candidate for membership with them and it wasn't right for me to take advantage of them either. The great wide world still lay out ahead of me and I'd make my own road through it without them. I went in and I said to the man there that I wanted to leave.

'You need to take a good, close look at yourself,' he said, 'and not make any rash decisions. You have a good outlook and spirit and to tell you the truth, you have a good light within you and you'll regret it, if you leave us.'

'Maybe I can see the light,' I says, 'but there are many stars in the sky. The draw of native tradition is a powerful thing. And as I sang last Sunday:

A Dhónaill, nach cuimhin leat le n-aithris
Mar tugadh an Ghlas Ghaibhleanna Mhór
Go Toraigh ar lorg a rubaill
Agus tháinig sí ar ais go tír mór?

Oh Dónall, don't you remember how to tell
The tale of An Glas Ghaibhleann Mhór
How she came to Tory in search of her own tail
And returned to the mainland once more?'

He didn't understand me however.

8

Tom Kerrigan called in the following day and we went out to Dún Laoghaire. We walked out by the West Pier and sat down on the flagstones there facing the sun. I told him what had happened between me and the Salvation Army. Tom was always afraid that I'd die of hunger.

'What'll you do now?' he says.

'As if I know! Just sun myself here for as long as I can – or whatever.'

'Do you know what you should do?' he says after a while. 'You should go down to Roscrea or Mount Melleray.[2] They'd put you up free of charge there for a good while.'

'That's not a bad idea,' I says, 'but I was thinking of something else.'

'Eli Ben Alim maybe?' he says.

Tom was forever going on about Eli Ben Alim.

'Eli Ben Alim has passed onto Conn's Halls in the next world by now,' I says, 'just as An Buinneán Donn is gone to his winter quarters. A man is coming who's more courageous than Eli, a man who's more far-seeing also. A shaft of light struck the flagstones here a few minutes ago as I was listening to the lapping of the waves. And I saw it as if in a dream – Parthalán[3] – the first man that ever came to Ireland. Parthalán was the first person to live in Donegal so you could say in all truth that he was a Donegal-man. I feel a special link with him as a consequence. Whenever I recall his achievements, I feel renewed. He came to Ireland and the chances are that he had no money or possessions worth talking about – nothing except his boat and his two oars and maybe a bit of a sail. And yet, he hit out into the wilderness of this foreign land completely alone. We can't travel twenty miles from home these days without cars to transport us and people serving us whatever we need and telling us where to go. And yet, despite all of this Parthalán – completely alone – founded an entirely new nation that is still here today. If I got up now and set out by boat from this place here and struck out in an easterly direction, who knows what great things might come out of it? And anyway, no matter what I do I'm planning on setting out into the world without money because I'm sick to death of it. Money is just a badge of identity that ignorant people use to connect with one another and to make everyone else as petty as themselves.'

'What you're saying is worth doing,' says Tom. 'It'd be no bother to steal a boat from the shore down there.'

'It's not that I want to imitate one of the characters in those stories they tell youngsters,' I says, and I was no longer addressing Tom now but the world in general and my own inner soul. 'Such an act isn't as crazy as it looks. When someone's nearly a year living on nothing, it begins to affect their mind. There's not a day's hardship that comes along from now on that I won't see as a failure and a hindrance to my imagination – if I don't mark it by undertaking great deeds that elevate me in my own eyes. It is just stupid for me to continue with this constant striving for money. The people with money threw me out the door and I can never go back in through that door again, it's so tightly guarded. But if I circle the fort the back way, I'll catch them unawares and it'll be a hundred times more satisfying when I get one over on them again – and I'll be a source of wonder to myself all the while. This here insight is Heaven-sent my son,' I says, 'and it's not every day that someone's blessed with it. Behind the scenes, they'll think that they have me beaten. And they threw me out and rejected me because they thought me too dangerous for them. And when Ceithearnach Caolriabhach Uí Dhónaill appears to them again and arrives in by the back door, they'll think he's lost it completely and he's just playing games. And no sooner am I back in with them again, but they'll be all happy and shaking hands with me and all the rest of it. And it won't matter what crazy things I get up to then as long as they appear to make sense. There's no doubt about it but you need to be a clever man to cross the Irish Sea in a small boat and I'd need to be plenty-cute too to make my way once I'm over there and on dry land too.'

'I know a place where it'd be easy to swipe a boat without anyone knowing,' says Tom.

'We'll need oars as well, you know,' I says. 'You'd be in a right bad way if you stole a boat without oars. We'll need to swipe the oars and hide them somewhere before we go home this evening and put a mark on the boat we've picked out.'

'Let's go,' says Tom and he was so delighted that you'd have sworn another sun had appeared in the sky, especially for him. We wandered our way along the shore and there were any number of boats there but needless to say, most of them were stationed close to where people could keep an eye on them. Next, we walked out as far as Grand Harbour.

'What do you think of this one?' Tom says.

'That one would be easy to move and beach,' I says, 'but it's only a little shell of a thing really. But here's one that's like the ones they have in the Donegal Gaeltacht, the ones the men have when they go out fishing to Boilg Chonaill, and there's no fear at all of them. It'd be heavy for one man to row by himself but we could stagger it so that we both row at different times. She's a sturdy vessel and she'll make it across if the weather doesn't break, or if we don't lose confidence in our own ability and strength. Do you see the name on her? The Mermaid. I like that but from now on we'll call her Leaving Ireland and nothing else – in honour of Colm Cille and our travels. And now, we'll go on a little bit further to find a pair of heavy oars – three oars if possible. It won't be easy to hide them either as there are always plenty of people down around here.'

'I know a place where there's a cave in beneath a hill,' says Tom. 'She goes right back into the hill and we were always in and out of it when we were children. They closed it up with small rocks since but I smashed a small hole into it last year. We can hide the oars there.'

'Fair play!' I says. 'You've put the icing on the cake for us with that. We'll leave the oars there and we'll wait in the cave tonight until it's a good time to leave. I'll get the oars and you can wait for me close to the mouth of the cave.'

Implementing our plan didn't prove as easy as I'd first thought however. As soon as I approached any boat, a man would appear and call out to me:

'Looking for a boat sir?'

'How much?' I'd say.

'A half-a-crown an hour.'

'Ah! We'll wait until the pound rises again!'

And if that happened to me once, it must have happened twenty times. I walked along surveying all the boats and eventually picked one out that nobody was watching over. I spent about a quarter of an hour pretending to do some work on her. I removed the cork and drained the water out of her, then turned her on her side, propped her up, and examined her from top to bottom. Eventually, I lifted the oars onto my shoulder and walked on. No one paid any heed to me and I went back to Tom, and we made our way out to the cave. That's when Tom showed me a sight that was truly magical. We went at least two hundred feet right into that cave and inside the heart of that hill, I shed a full ten years' weight off my shoulders and I felt as young as Tom himself once more.

'I forgot one thing,' I says. 'We'd be better off bringing some food with us. Do you think we could break into a bread van somewhere?'

'Hang on,' says Tom. 'My family share a big shop with another business and I can swipe whatever food we need from there – bread and fish, and salmon and apples and eggs and all that.'

'And a few bottles of milk,' I says. 'We'll need water as well. They say that fresh water is always what boat-men need the most. We'll come back here at nine o'clock. I'll have a small bag with me for our stuff.'

Back home that evening, I ate a tiny bit of food that I had in, and smoked a cigarette, the last one I had left. I got two pairs of socks, a razor, a shirt, a bit of glass mirror, a sliver of soap and put them all into a small bundle. Next thing, I thought of going out for a walk around the streets that I was so familiar with. I quickly copped onto myself again however.

Hang on! Hang on! I says to myself. If I'm planning on rowing during the night, I'm better off having a rest now. I lay down and stretched out, and read a book. I read a story as fine as was ever told. It was about a man who escaped from prison in the West Indies using a small boat. He lived in a castle owned by a gentleman for a time, and all the while they were besieged by various local looters and pirates. The lord was killed and on the day of the funeral, the young man and the gentleman's daughter ran away secretly and made for the small boat. The whole story had a really poetic atmosphere about it. Not only could you see the gentleman's coffin as clear as day but you imagined the monk's passing through the chapel and the high altar festooned with candles. You saw all of this as clearly as if you'd been present yourself – or more clearly still.

You understood how moving and incredible it was to follow this path down through the underground passage at the back of this church and this surly dark Spaniard leading the way for you. You knew that this story was worth gold and a great deal more – its words – how that small creaking timber boat emerged warily from the shallows. And there was a mist on the sea and a boatful of pirates hidden out in the heart of it playing music on Spanish harps punctuated with the occasional sound of the oars. This world of mine lingered somewhere between sleep and waking and bounded within the unfathomable expanse of each tiny living moment – until the last rays of sun had faded on the fields. And it was only then that I remembered the boat I'd take to the water with me was not my own.

And I sensed in that moment that this world was hostile and indifferent to me now that I was setting out on my adventure. On the tram, the people's faces seemed smug and satisfied as if they had a true knowledge of this world that could never be mine. And how often has this chilled me to the bone – that superior and self-assured look on people's faces when even the smallest thing is enough to make them contented – these people so urban that they would disgust you and they all jammed together in rows, like little sardines stuck in boxes.

Passing out by Blackrock, however, an old man from the country got onto the tram and you'd have known he was a man of the land even if half of him was gone. He wore a blue suit, needless to say, and the two big swollen hands on him, and the cap tipped sideways on his forehead. He was twisted-drunk. He sat down and started to sing and sway in his seat.

I couldn't hear what he was saying. It was just a rough mumble but eventually I made out the following words clearly:

> *We've handled sword and gun,*
> *Fighting every nation's battle but our own.*

And then he repeated that murmuring croon of his again until he came to the same words in the song, and he sang them out with a power that reverberated from the roof of the tram.

'Health and long life to you!' I says. 'Where were you earlier when we needed you?'

Tom was waiting for me when I got there. He never liked being late for anything and I didn't ask him whether he was sad to be leaving his people behind. He had a torch in his hand and he went into the cave ahead of me, and we searched around until we saw the outline of the oars where we'd left them earlier.

'We've plenty of time,' I says. 'We're better off not moving from here until the trams come to a stop. Do you have everything?'

'I do indeed,' he says, and we sat there at the mouth of the cave, chatting from time to time, and watching the lights far away and the cars streaking past and their enormous shadows in the dark. The night was so still that if the branches of a tree had stirred, you'd have sworn it had done so of its own volition. A quarter of moon stood eastwards above the sea, its light draping the earth. The Kish lighthouse flashed on and off out at the edge of the horizon. Tom showed me an old pistol he'd brought with him. It must have been eighty years old and a handful of stones would have been more useful, but he claimed that he could still do damage with it. I showered him with praise for his youthful exuberance and for the sake of every outlaw of the woods or pirate that ever lived – when this world was still full of poetry.

'It's no harm having that on you,' I says.

Those three hours we spent at the mouth of the cave were rich in inspiration, each and every moment as alive as the great tears that form the rainbow or the motes within a ray of sun. The cave funnelled deep and dark behind us as we made our way right into the heart of the hill and the shoreline down below us and the great city within us, and the hundreds and thousands of ordinary people whose only concern was getting to sleep. There were guards within shouting distance of us who'd have been delighted to have nabbed us, but we were free of them – and yet we didn't know from one minute to the next when we might run into them in the darkness. It was after midnight when we propelled Leaving Ireland down the shingle and set her stern to the waves. The sea was as quiet as a mountain lake as we made our way out along the headland and across Dalkey Sound unnoticed by any living thing.

'How long will it take us to get across?' says Tom.

'If we could keep going at the pace we're doing now,' I says, 'we should make it across within twenty-four hours.

The hardest thing for us is that we can't travel across in a straight line exactly. But it won't take us long. This sea here is a piece of cake.'

Privately, I knew well that we wouldn't make it across within twenty-four hours. There were strong currents ahead and if there was any wind at all, we'd lose a lot of time and Tom was a bad rower and wouldn't have the stamina to keep going till morning. But none of this mattered; at least we were on our way.

'Don't worry son,' I says. 'We'll get Leaving Ireland over by this time tomorrow.'

We left Dalkey like a black hillock behind us and we sailed out past the headland. Once we had another mile done, we were warming up and the shoreline was gradually disappearing from view. By the second mile, we'd settled down into the long, steady rhythm of the waves. We went on and the great expanse of the sea stretched out in front of us so that there was nothing to be seen except for the odd light. Once we'd been about two hours rowing, I let my oars drift for a moment.

'Take a breather,' I says to Tom. Tom was nearly wiped out by then anyway even if there was no hint of him taking a break and no point in me telling him to relax either.

'Do you see where the Kish lighthouse is now?' I says. 'We've rowed strongly but there's no way we could keep this pace up for twenty-four hours. Do you have a cigarette?'

We lit up and smoked, and took our ease. Tom put his hand over the gunwale and dipped it into the brine but withdrew it as quickly again.

'It's damn cold,' he says.

'Colder than you'd think,' I says. 'How are the palms of your hands holding up?'

'They're bad enough,' he says.

I looked at them and they were already very red and raw looking.

'Never mind that,' I says, 'that's lack of practice. They'll be toughening up as you go along.'

My own hands were only average as well.

'I'll put my pocket handkerchief over them,' he says.

'Don't,' I says. 'You're better off without it. Stick them in the water and wet your oars then.'

We kept going. We started chatting after a short while and we were so engrossed in the conversation that we barely noticed a ship coming in our direction. It passed us by and it was as big as a mountain with one hundred eyes and the wash from it set Leaving Ireland bobbing all over the place. We watched its lights disappear from us as it made its way towards Dublin.

'Pity that you have no bullets in that pistol,' I says.

'I have powder,' he says. 'I'll give it a go.' He stood up in the stern and fired. The pistol gave a small damp flash, like striking a match on rock but the noise it made was as nothing out there in the middle of the ocean. That said, I found it fairly funny enough!

We were very tired come daybreak and I was sure that we weren't even halfway across by then. I was waiting for the sun to rise so that I could witness the spectacle of it. The air freshened and it seemed to me that the wind sharpened also and after another while, the sun came up. The sky reddened in an easterly direction and she lit up the entire sea. We had a bite to eat and set to again. We began to take turns at the rowing and I found that this wasn't half as brutal as what we'd been doing earlier. It wasn't easy for me to make much headway with Tom however.

'The morning's not as clean as it should be,' I says. 'What's the bets the weather's going to break?'

'Sure, we're nearly across now,' says Tom.

'Oh, take it handy son!' I says. 'It's a wide channel.'

A half an hour later and the sky grew dark as if someone had pulled the blinds down over it. Rain began to fall in drops as big as spoons and thunder exploded and lightning flashed across the sky. The wind swirled around us and the sea rose in a way that put the heart crossways in me.

'Keep her mouth in the wind Tom.'

But it didn't matter what I did, he was letting her spin around and I didn't know from one minute to the next whether we might go under. I took the oars back off him.

'If we even had a small bit of ballast in, or a piece of sail itself, we could really get moving,' I says. 'It would still be dangerous enough though as I'm not too well up on sailing. We'll go on another bit anyway.'

The storm continued to swirl around us and I understood properly in that moment just how treacherous the sea can be, even at the nicest time of the year. And the Irish Sea is dirty and squally when she's disturbed. A half hour later and I was fighting with all the pride and strength left in my body. We were both soaked to the skin from the rain and we were taking a small amount of water aboard as well.

'If this continues, she's going to fill up on us. Bail for your life you bitch – as hard and as fast as you can. We'll have to turn her around somehow, I'm afraid.'

Thomas was white in the face by then and he couldn't talk. I could tell by then that we wouldn't make it back to shore again on time. I managed to turn her around and keep her straight before the wind as best I could. Tom was useless at this stage. He had no strength left in his arms and he couldn't row at all; I kept pulling and pulling on the oars until my wrists went numb and there was no relief at all. Every now and then, Tom would shout over that he'd take his turn on the oars but I'd call back:

'Stay where you are or we'll capsize.'

The storm roared for another hour and then it fell calm and the day lit up.

'Oh King of Glory!' I said 'we were alright in the end. This here is the best boat ever; we were never going to go down. We're safe now but I'm afraid that we're not going to make it across – not this time anyway. I'm nearly dead. Here, take the oars now and don't forget that there's still a strong current there. Don't let the oars go too deep in the water and don't miss your stroke at the crest of the wave or you'll be thrown backwards.'

It was six o'clock in the morning by then but it was nearly eight o'clock by the time we saw land.

'God bless you Ireland!' I said 'I don't know whether that's Howth or Lambay Island. It looks too low to be Howth. But if it was Dún Rámha Island we could make port and have a rest.'

It was Lambay and we had to fight hard to reach it. The afternoon sun was at its height by then and we stretched ourselves out on the grass verge and slept till late evening.

A large group of women were swimming in the shallows by the quayside near the West Pier and they barely noticed our small boat as it passed them around four o'clock and came ashore between them and Malahide Beach.

9

Any doubts I harboured that we shouldn't have turned around and returned home were laid to rest that night. I was lying in bed listening to the wind and rain lashing the window and the gale screaming and tearing through the city and me thinking that my little boat would have been useless if I'd been out on the waves then and if I hadn't managed to turn her around and get her back to shore again. I went into the city centre the following morning and on my way in, it came to me that it'd be terrible not to return the boat to whoever owned it at Grand Harbour. So I went into a shop and bought a stamp and wrote this note at the base of Nelson's Pillar:

To the Officer at Dalkey Barracks.
    Dear fair-haired, young lad – If you've received a complaint that a boat named The Mermaid was stolen

from Grand Harbour on the night of the 17th you can find it in on the shore in Howth directly across from the Claremont Hotel. Written on the top of Nelson's Tower on the 19th of the month of the Corn Marigold, 1933, by me, the Erring Son, who's under a vow not to state his name. Up De Valéra forever!

I managed to get access to a typewriter for a few minutes in a house I regularly visited and printed the letter up without anyone noticing. I posted it in the GPO then and I felt relieved afterwards. I received some money just after this, a payment I hadn't been expecting to come for a long time. I had a book in with An Gúm at the time but I'd thought that I wouldn't hear anything about it for another three months at least. I'd sent it onto them only half-heartedly – to see what they'd do with it. They'd accepted it. Also, on top of this, I received six pounds and twenty in wages that I'd earned two years previous to this and that hadn't been paid to me at the time.

I'll go to Algiers, I says to myself. I'll go and see the French Legion and the dark Arabs of the sand dunes. I spent two days dreaming about such adventures. Then it came to me that I'd miss a lot on my journey east and I decided to go to London in the end. There were things in London that I wanted to see, especially Turner's paintings.

When I found myself alone in London I felt really low and depressed however. This time, I didn't articulate it in any way and remained silent instead. And the worst thing of all about it was that I couldn't see what had caused it. I was used to walking around Dublin and I couldn't put the streets of that city out of my mind, but London's streets were three times as long and I found myself dead-tired every after-noon. The smoke and the noise and the high buildings got me down and after I'd been there a fortnight, I got sick of it. And yet even within that short space of time one of life's many wonders came my way.

One day I was passing a pub in a backstreet and I felt thirsty and I went in. There were only three people inside, two of whom left a few minutes later. It seems to be a strange trait of mine that people who find themselves in trouble make a bee-line for me and talk to me about it. I was drinking my bottle of beer and minding my own business when the sole customer left there approached me. He crept over to me like a frightened mouse eluding the mighty cat.

'I'm sorry for bothering you,' he says, 'but you have the look of an honest man about you.'

'All I know about that is that a man from my native county told a Frenchman once that Ireland had raised at least one honest person anyway – when she raised me. I only heard back what he'd said by accident afterwards but I'm glad that I contradicted those words in the Bible that say no man is a prophet in his own land.'

'I see,' he says, then spoke in a whisper: 'I'm the man that the dope gangs of America are after.'

'Just as well for me that we ran into each other,' I says. 'I'm the man that Eve's Seed is after.'

But he had no interest in what I said; he was intent on telling me about himself and nothing else. Where's the man who doesn't like the sound of his own voice, I thought? And God knows but he had a strange story to tell too.

'Robert Murray is my name,' he says, 'I was born in Glasgow. As a boy, I went to work in a small shop but I was only about a year there when I got sick of it. I often hung around the docks as I have seafaring blood in me, and one day I put my name down for a ship that was travelling to New York. Once we'd dropped anchor across the water, I jumped ship. I went to a lodging house frequented by sailors and met a fellow there the likes of whom I'd never met before. This man was the soul of generosity and he brought me around to all the pubs, cafés and music halls and showed me all the fun and hotspots of the city. And he paid the bills everywhere we went. I was young and a bit afraid of his type and so I kept my senses about me at all times. One day he told me that he'd been observing me for a while and that I was a good, shrewd lad and that he was thinking of arranging a job for me that would put tons of money in my direction. He brought me to a shop in one of the poor back-streets and I met a man there who was very friendly to me also. He said he'd give me a job on another ship again but that I wouldn't be entirely reliant on this job for a living – that I'd also get 500 dollars on top of my wages for every trip I made. All I had to do was deliver parcels of opium from one place to another. I'd often read stories about such deals and they'd got a hold on my imagination and I agreed to do the work for these men. They put me on board a ship going to Le Havre and I was ordered to go to a particular house there to collect the opium. The pick-up went smoothly and the parcel wasn't very big. I carried the opium in my pockets and brought it to a shop in a New York where I was paid my 500 dollars. I worked away like this until the end of the year by which time I had thousands of dollars put away. Then they sent me on a boat to Hamburg and that transport was even easier than the previous one. All the while the American law enforcement people were looking for our entire gang however. They didn't catch any of us in the act but eventually they'd had us under surveillance for so long that I was the main suspect for moving the opium and other drugs coming in from Hamburg. One day we were hiding down by the docks when a man handed me a coin with three holes in it. This was a sign that they were on my tail. I only just about managed to hide the parcel of drugs before the police officers raided the boat. They searched the vessel from top to bottom but didn't find anything. When I landed that day I was told that it was too dangerous for me to continue transporting the drugs by boat and that I'd be put on a train and make the deliveries from New York to Chicago from then on. This worked fine for a good while. No one paid much heed to a man on a train carrying a small bag. And I had one big advantage that the average manual labourer didn't have. I didn't have to do heavy work and wear old or dirty clothes so that I had a respectable look about me and my choice of food and drink. I was four years on this drug route until I nearly became immune to the fact that I was involved in a very dangerous game. One day, I was eating my dinner in the food car when I fell asleep. I just leaned my head back on the seat and conked out. When I woke up I had a headache. I didn't pay much heed to this at first and I don't know what came over me but after a short while, I decided to check my bag. It was empty! I'd lost 40,000 dollars, an incredible amount of money, and there was no way I could go back to the bosses and tell them this, I was too afraid of them. And I knew then why I'd fallen asleep so suddenly and why I'd got the headache. They'd put something in the food to make me dopey. It was a disaster. There was no way I could go back and face the bosses. Anyone who lost a delivery – they'd give them the bullet and get rid of them straight away. I sat there on the train to Chicago so petrified that I couldn't move. Eventually, I spotted the city lights ahead and I pulled myself together and left the train before it landed at Central Station. I left Chicago that night on a different train. I never stayed anywhere for long after this but kept moving until, in the end, I'd travelled halfway around the world. And there's no town I've spent the night in that I didn't expect to feel the cold mouth of a pistol shoved into my back at some point. I've spent most of my money at this stage and all I can do is keep running as best I can. They'll catch me some day though.'

'Do you know what you should do now?' I says. 'Go to Ireland.'

'Go to Ireland!' he says, and you'd have thought from the way he said it that he was more afraid of the Irish than he was of the drug gangs!

'Yes. All you'd have to do is join one of the political parties there. You won't be in one of them a month, needless to say, before someone will say that you were working for the drugs gangs in America but you'd have nothing to worry about – no one would believe this anyway. Because everyone involved in politics is slandered in some way or another. And if they didn't accuse you of that, they'd say your grandfather was a poultry-thief or something. Then, if any of your pursuers came after you, all you'd have to do is go on the run. You'd have the look of a gentleman about you, and there wouldn't be any reward for you, and I doubt if there's many men in Chicago who could track you down. And if you were captured over in Ireland and put in prison, you'd be grand. You were once the leader of a drug gang and everyone would be afraid of their lives to put a bullet in you because they'd think you still had your gang over in the United States. And the worst thing that could happen to you is that the authorities hung you or shot you. And even then, thousands would come to your funeral and they'd make speeches over your coffin and remember you until your tomb fell to ruin.'

He stared at me for a few seconds.

'Where are you stopping?' he says.

'Number 3, Cleopatra's Needle,' I says.

He'd never heard of the Needle before as it turns out and he believed me.

'I might pay you a visit sometime,' he says.

'Sure! Call around tomorrow.' I says. 'And don't worry your head about the crowd with the pistols. There are plenty of ways to kill someone – from the belly to the ear.'

I didn't bother my head about him after that. I couldn't help him anyway. His fear of his enemies meant that he couldn't forgive himself for what he'd done. But his fear of them also meant that he couldn't forget them either. I've never had much sympathy for corrupt people who find themselves in trouble however because I know that they'd be the ruin of me too if they got half the chance.

I wasn't that bothered about him at all. And I had my own worries to deal with anyway. The streets were making me depressed and claustrophobic. I'll keep moving and travel on as far as Algiers, I thought to myself. But then it came to me one day that I'd left another country out of the equation that few Irish people knew much about – Wales. There were hills in that country and when I considered this, my heart was filled with longing. A unique language was spoken there, a language that people knew very little about, a living language, and she was spoken much more widely than was Irish. Wouldn't it be lovely to get to know more about her!

What was the point of me following the same wide road that everyone else followed, I thought. That wasn't my way. I wasn't going to discover my destiny by taking the same road as everyone else – the way of the cars and boats. And only an ignorant person would be happy to admit that they'd never been to Wales. Wander the roads that no one else wanders, in God's name, even if it's only to see the chicken-houses along the way.

I'd heard it said before that Liverpool was the capital city of North Wales, and that this was the least anglicized part of that country and so I struck out for Liverpool. I found out then that it was as easy to go from Liverpool to Wales as to travel from Galway town to Connemara.

10

I liked Liverpool. Each to their own opinion, but I thought it was a nicer city than London. The streets were laid out better and the heart of the city was as fine as you could ask for anywhere and there was a view from the riverbank down there as striking and as beautiful as you'd find in any city in the world.

I stayed in lodgings there not far from the river. I found the lodgings fairly easily and it suited me grand. I don't like lodgings that are too big. They're not peaceful enough and they're not social enough either. After all, the nest is never bigger than the bird and a dwelling house should never be that big that it makes someone anxious or uneasy. There are certain buildings that should be big of course – churches and court-houses, for example. But such buildings are built for the purposes of the soul and the intellect, and not for the human being's physical requirements.

I checked in and ordered a good meal and sat down in the café there. There were a good many people in the room and they were very quiet. I compared this silently in my mind with other countries that I knew something about. In cafés in France, everyone's chatting. In cafés in Ireland, people are quiet but you wouldn't be surprised if someone struck up a conversation with you. But in England, the people are quiet, so quiet that you'd imagine they'd never utter a word. It just goes to show – he has conquered half of the world and yet the Englishman remains an anxious individual beneath it all. And maybe there's nothing wrong with that either. These are real, true English people I thought to myself. Kind, moderate people and with nothing in the way of show or pretence about them. People for whom the sound of someone cursing aloud would come as a shock to them. And they were all the one in their manner too – except for one lad who was sitting over near the wall and a fair-haired girl at the table next to him. They're Irish, I says to myself. They were bigger boned and lively looking and they didn't look as reserved as everyone else there. It's not that all of the Irish are bigger people than the English but normally they're stronger looking and have healthier complexions, and they have a different look about them completely.

It was true for me. I wasn't there long I when I heard the blonde girl and the boy talking. It was as if they were performing a drama the way they went on. I've noticed that Irish people talk like this when they are abroad; I think all the Irish do it to one extent or another. This girl was very chatty and loved talking and you knew by her that she had a lively mind and that she still had a certain innocence about her. She's one of those people, I thought, who's curious about the world and wants to know everything about other people – just as her exact opposite would be someone who couldn't be bothered talking to anyone else.

She was a beautiful-looking woman – for sure – and there was nothing shy or hesitant about her. It wasn't long before she turned to me and said:

'You've a lonely look about you there?'

'I haven't seen any ghosts recently mind you,' I says, 'not unless you'd call one of the dream-women the poets met in their vision-poems long ago a ghost.'

'Are you from Ireland?' she says.

'I'm as Irish as the waters of the Boyne.'

'I'm from up north myself,' she says, '… I'm from Derry.' I can still remember most of our conversation word-for-word. A quarter of an hour later, I was reading her hand and telling her fortune and we'd completely forgotten where we were. Whatever it was anyway, this girl was keen on me. I've never gone out with any girl for more than a month. This doesn't mean that I don't like their company at times – particularly when I haven't many worries on my mind. I don't think it's true that the poets were always womanizers either. The way I see it a poet and a woman wouldn't have the patience to stay together for three months. And it's the men who are always killing themselves earning money that the women often have the most time for. And even if it is the poets who have described women in the sweetest and most beautiful ways, they have been maligned all the same.

Cé nach labhraim bím ag meabhrú go mór fá mo chroí,
Is tú mo chéadsearc agus ní féidir mo chumha a chloí.

Even though I do not speak I meditate greatly in my
*   heart,*
You are my first love and my parting sorrow cannot be
*   assuaged.*

Anyway, I was really cracked about this fine thing. And
I wouldn't mind – but I had competition from a young
Greek, a man from the land of Helen, the same crowd who
destroyed the Trojans. She told me that she'd been barely a
week in that lodgings when the Greek fellow was over to
her and always chatting her up in his broken English. And
he telling her that he liked Irish girls, and her especially. But
since my arrival, he hadn't tried it on with her apparently.
I think the poor devil realized that he wasn't one of us. As
it turned out, the lodgings-man wasn't that easy to put off
the scent however and it wasn't love that he was after either.
He was kind and friendly and but one look at him and the
biggest fool in the world would have kept their distance. He
was tall, thin and dark skinned but it wasn't as if he was
incredibly handsome or anything; and he had a pronounced
lower lip like you might see on a wild animal that was about
to take a bite out of you. That said, he was friendly to me, the
same as to everyone else. He brought the pair of us upstairs
to the sitting room. There was a sword and a bayonet on
the hearth where you'd normally find the rod and the spit. I
picked them up and had a good look at them. The bayonet
was French and the sword was German.

'Maybe he was in the Great War,' I says.

'He was,' she says, 'and he brought them home from the fighting.'

'I'd say he did alright!' I says. 'If I know anything, he stole these – for sure.'

'Oh well, at least he's a nice man anyway,' she says. 'He's very nice to me. I don't like his wife at all but he brought me down a cup of tea himself yesterday – and he asked me to give him my money so that he could put it in a box for me, for safekeeping.'

'There's nothing wrong with the tea,' I says, 'but if I was you, I'd keep a close eye on my money.'

'He's a hard worker,' she says, backing him. 'He was only a driver once and look at him now – he's after buying this big house here.'

'If he gets many others to put their money in his box for safekeeping,' I says, 'he won't be long buying up half the city.'

He arrived into the room just after I'd said this, and we began talking.

'I like this city, it's not noisy and stressful at all,' I says.

'It isn't,' he says, knowingly.

'Everyone's fairly relaxed and easy-going. This here must be one of the biggest streets in the city and there are lots of Irish names on the shops around here.'

'Oh, there must be at least a hundred thousand Irish people in this city. How are things in Ireland these days?' he says.

'Things are quiet enough in Ireland at the moment,' I says, 'other than in the newspapers.'

'That's the truth, I'd imagine,' he says.

I don't know what got into me to bring this up because I never usually discuss the ancient conflict which Strongbow kicked off years ago with anyone from England. That said, this man had a fine, sensible outlook on the issue. The girl kept interrupting the conversation however; maybe she didn't feel included enough in it.

'I'm always slagging him off about his hat,' she says, pointing at me.

I was sporting a green hat that I'd bought in Dublin, one that was in fashion that year. I wasn't sure whether an Englishman might think a green hat the likes of this was a cultural thing relating to the Gaeltacht or Irish nationalism or relating to something military possibly. There was no fear that your man was this stupid however.

'That's a good hat,' he says. 'I get my hats from the same people.'

You're polite anyway, I'll say that much for you, I thought. Be that as it may, I still wouldn't put my money in your savings-box.

He left a short while later and went downstairs to the café again.

'What do you think of him anyway?' she says.

'He's a man that I'd like,' I says, 'if the world was as it should be. He's got some good points but he's as cunning as all the devils of hell and he'd rob you blind quicker than you'd tie your shoelaces. He's bred from the city's tenements but he's never suffered hardship in his life. I'd say he was probably in the war alright and that he was a good soldier. He's got plenty of go in him but he's mad for money. And this life is so tough that he'll never have an ounce of honesty or truth in him.'

'That's what I think as well,' she says, 'except I didn't let on anything to him. There's something about this house that's unhappy.'

A young girl came in then carrying a small kitten and she started showing the cat to the Irish girl. Right in the middle of the conversation, she says,

'My father was only joking, you know, when he asked you to put your money in the box!'

I was stunned at this. You can never underestimate how shrewd children can be. There's no flies on this one, I said to myself. Later on, the girl and I went out to the pictures and when we were coming home, she turned the conversation around to the Greek again.

'He often works in a small room at the top of the stairs,' she says, 'in a sort of an office he has there. The lodgers have to pass through it whenever they come and go from their rooms. He has some kind of a printing machine there and he's always using it.'

'The next time you're up there have a good scout at it,' I says.

Later, when I was getting my tea, she came in and sat down beside me at the table.

'I passed him earlier and saw him working the machine,' she says. 'He puts a piece of paper in one side of it and it comes out the other as a ten-shilling note.'

'Well, by my seven souls, but you're really onto something there,' I says. 'I can see his game now. He puts these notes into circulation by passing them out amongst his customers any time he gets a chance. And for every person who spots that they're false there are probably plenty of others he sent on their way with empty pockets – and they never even realized it.'

'They should get the law after him,' she says.

'I don't know,' I says. 'It's their job to catch him, not ours. I don't have anything against him. It takes guts for a man to get up to the likes of that. And there's something kind of innocent about someone who plays tricks like that too – and it'll catch up with them eventually anyway. He was probably honest enough starting out in life; usually the likes of him start out as honest. But most people haven't it in them to profit in such a way. The first thing that tipped me off to the fact that there was a certain element of manliness and humanity about him was this – he doesn't have strong views on anything. Always be on your guard against someone who's too good to be true; because you'll find out someday that underneath that nice side of them lies nothing but greed in reality. The innocent man is the one who can speak at least one word of the truth. But there are others who are incapable of telling the truth – there sure are – and some of them aren't that far away from me either to tell you the truth. Here's how you'll always know them; they always have a great public image and reputation about them. I'd advise you to steer clear of him and let him hang himself. The Saviour was hanged between two criminals and if he'd been waiting to be tortured between two honest men, He might still be here in this world.'

We both left that place the following day, with me heading for Wales and the girl moving on to a different lodgings. She was looking for work. In fact, she had another job lined up and was just waiting for the go-ahead to begin work there. She had her own way of finding the next job too. She'd enter the biggest shop in the city and make a beeline for the boss himself. She'd ignore anyone else who approached her and spoke only to whoever was the boss. And by the time she was finished talking to him, he'd have promised her a job – guaranteed. And this was even if he'd got rid of other people only the previous week. She was an amazing girl that way. Growing up, her family had been reasonably well-off and they'd sent her to the best of schools. But she hadn't learned anything much. Certain things came easily to her by nature but education wasn't one of them. Her father and mother had died young and she'd been raised by her relatives. When she was older, she'd fallen out with them and accused them of being too controlling. She left home and spent a number of years working in different parts of Ireland. She'd found herself in Belfast around November 1932, when the poor of the city had revolted. She was working in a hotel at the time and she joined in the protests and smashed plates and other things on the premises. When the trouble began later again, she'd moved to Dublin for work but, as she admitted to me when we were chatting, she'd had enough of Dublin by this point. If the people of Belfast had been as rough as the people in Dublin, then the latter city would've been destroyed and reduced to rubble years ago, she said. Each to their own opinion as I mentioned earlier. She'd found work in Dublin but after a while she'd got fed-up with it and came over to England. I said my goodbyes to her and wished her all the best. But many's the time afterwards that I thought of my Macha Mongrua[1] as this was the name I'd given her privately. There's no doubt but that she had some of the same traits as the heroine who took over the tribe of Diotharba and who constructed the great fort at Eamhain long ago.

I travelled westwards through Wales then and walked a good deal of that country. I've related in another book what I learned about this small, strange country that is off the beaten track and that unique tribe of people – older than the Romans themselves – who inhabit it and I won't repeat it again now here.

11

Come winter, I found myself in Cardiff, down on the coast near Glamorgan, the place where they have the coal-fields. Although the city of Cardiff was the biggest coal port in the world prior to the First World War and a lot of coal still passes through it, you wouldn't know it from how the city looks today. It's a city full of fine shops, a wealthy and prosperous city. And there's no human inclination or desire – whether wise or foolish – that people don't profit from it. You see the fortune-tellers working in their offices along some of the finest streets of this city. I'd have had plenty of scope for this crack in Dublin but in this city here, I'd only have been wasting my time trying to compete with people who were well-established for years and had their money made already – and had probably become wealthy on the back of it too. Indeed, I have a card belonging to one of these very people in my pocket now as I'm writing this. And the following is printed in fine letters on it:

DR. ROBERT SCOTT-McGLADE,
Professional Psychologist

There is a street in Cardiff with so many butchers that they organize a weekly meat auction but the most disappointing thing for me was the bookshops. I'd had the habit of going into bookshops in Dublin and sometimes I'd spend a couple of hours reading a book in one of them. When I tried to do this in a shop in Cardiff however, they were straight over to greet me and I had no choice but to disappear in case they tried to sell me half of the shop. No one should be a bookseller if they've no understanding of books. It's important to mention here that there was a Welsh-language bookshop there and they weren't half as greedy as the others.

There were people from all four corners of the globe living in the city of Cardiff. I came across the solid and polite Englishman and the sudden, moody Welshman, and the forceful yet soft-hearted Scotsman, and the rough and cheeky Irishman; and the bright and intellectual Frenchman and the wild and animated Italian and the Greek who's somewhere between the last two; the yellow man who's inscrutable and neat, and the black man who's easy-going or sullen. There are churches of every faith there. I remember going into a Greek church one day to see what it was like. The walls were decorated very beautifully and the altar was in the centre of the room – if indeed it was an altar, as it looked more like a sideboard in a dining room at first glance. I saw people going in and out and blessing themselves on the forehead and the shoulders and everywhere on the upper half of the body and bowing down at this side altar and kissing silver statues and blessing themselves again while others sat around by the walls. This church was like the middle of a house and I couldn't really make much sense of it.

But speaking of places of worship, the strangest one of all that I came across was a spiritualist chapel. As many people know, a large number of English people believe that they can contact the spirits of the dead. I don't believe in this superstitious stuff at all and even if I did, that old saying would have had me on my guard: 'Leave forbidden things alone and they cannot harm you.' But the lodging-house woman convinced me to go to one of these spiritualist chapels anyway. Needless to say, I had to make conversation with her sometimes and she'd turned the conversation around to spiritualism before I even knew what was happening. She said that a big Native American man from the United States used to visit her from the otherworld with messages for her. And she told me that she was certain that I too had the ability to communicate with spirits and that I should accompany her to a spiritualist temple in the city some evening. Maybe it's worth going, I says to myself, even if it's only to keep her happy and who knows – maybe her cooking might improve a little bit as well. So I accompanied her one night, as gallant as a knight; this same woman was heavy and as round as a barrel and nearly fifty years of age. We went into a small hall that was only half-full and she went over to the organ and started to play and the congregation started up with the following hymn:

God send the power just now,
And thy children they will come
To carry the tidings home,
God send the power just now!

When they were finished with the music an old hag of a woman with the look of a sorcerer about her stood up and read an excerpt from the Bible after which they turned off the lights. I couldn't see anything in the room except for the enormous shapes reflected in the half-light from the street outside. All was peaceful on either side of me; next thing, I thought I heard someone sigh in a voice so low that the human ear could barely hear it. Then the dark and mysterious fairy queen spoke:

'I have a message for you,' she says pointing at someone across from me. 'The spirit that left us last November is asking you not to worry at all and not to have any doubts about the year ahead. He says that you'll be going to London in the summer but that you shouldn't forget to visit someone who is living in such-and-such a street. He'll tell you the name of the house and who this person is once he has spoken to them. You don't know each other at all at present but you will do within three weeks.'

She passed on various messages here and there to people scattered around the room and eventually she sat down again. Then a black man who was beside me got to his feet. I'd noticed this man just after coming in. He was a placid-looking fellow and reasonably tall with wide shoulders as is common to his people and his body was light and lithe looking. Just after I'd arrived in, he'd got up to open the door for someone. As he rose to his feet however, a white man had tried to take his seat but I'd swiped the chair straight away before he could do so. This lout had turned on me then but I issued a powerful Irish curse in a half-whisper and frightened him off. I gave the black man the chair again and he was very grateful to me. The poor fellow was so shocked that a white man had shown him any kindness, that for a moment he didn't know whether to sit or stand. Rising to his feet however, he indicated to the gathering that he had dark powers that few others possessed. A wave of tension swept through the gathering as he spoke. I don't know what went through the minds of the people he passed on messages to – but you could tell by them that he was striking home with every word he uttered. His voice was deep and sad and had a strange tone to it in the darkness of that large room. Next he spoke to me:

'You're different from the others gathered here tonight. Your mind is on other things and you are travelling a different road. I can see a long, lonely walk ahead of you before you leave this country again. You work for the newspapers and you are currently writing a book. You sent a book to certain people and it's still under review with one man favouring the book and three against it. This isn't the book that'll set you up however and neither is it the second one – but rather the third one instead.'

I nearly believed in spiritualism after that. I'd never met this man before and he didn't know anything about me; and neither had he any experience of literature or writers' lives and yet despite this, everything he said to me was true. In fact, the third book – the one that he said would make my name – is the one I'm currently writing. Once the magic was done and people were going home, I approached the black man and spoke with him. We walked down the street together and he told me a bit about his life. He'd been brought up in the West Indies and had spent a while in the United States before moving to England. He'd been living in Cardiff for the previous year surviving on the money that the state gives men who are out of work. His name was Matthews. I asked him to call around to me for a chat the next night he was free and he said that he'd come around the following evening. Maybe the poor man thought that he'd landed on his feet after meeting me and it almost turned out this way too – but more about this in due course. He called around the next evening and we had a long night of chat. This was the first time I'd ever got to know a black person and I didn't get a bad impression of such people at all. He was quiet-spoken and polite and had a nice way about him, and a good sense of humour to boot. He was bright and had a particular talent for reading people's minds. He told me the story of his life.

'I was born in the West Indies. My father was a white man. At school, I was the best child in the class. One day the inspector came around. He spoke to me and told me that I was very bright.

"But what good is that you?" he says, "as you won't get anything out of it. You'd be as well off staying at home. You're black and you'll be kept down."

'When I went home that evening I ran into my father and said

"Why the hell did you marry my mother?" He stared at me momentarily and said

"Because that's life, darling. Don't you know that I have the height of respect for your mother?"

"But the inspector told me that I've no future ahead of me because I'm black and if you hadn't married my mother then I wouldn't be black, would I?"

"Curse him!" says my father! "He was some man putting my son down like that, wasn't he?"

'He called to the inspector and they were very rough with each other, and my father laid him out with one punch of his fist. I watched the whole thing but said nothing. I was black and they were white, and I left it between themselves.

'On leaving school, I got a job in a motor garage. It was a rotten job and very badly paid and all I got was threepence a day. Eventually I left and went to America and when I saw the terrible way my people are treated over there, it often set me thinking that there was no God. If I told you about all the places I've wandered since first arriving in Cardiff, I'd be talking for a week. And there's nowhere I've been that I didn't find my people oppressed and treated like dirt – and none of us understanding why things were this way.

'There are old people back home who still remember when a black man could be bought for a penny. We're still not worth very much today. They say that we're wild and uncivilized but they forget that Egypt is the most ancient nation in the world. They forget what colour skin Jesus Christ had and if He was the same as the people He was raised with, then his skin wasn't very white. We did our part of the fighting during the First World War and spilled plenty of our blood but on returning home, we got little thanks for it. A white man will get ten shillings a week in this city if he's destitute but a black man will only get eight. All I get is myself is six shillings a week.'

'Have the Black People any hope of being granted their rights any time soon?' I says.

'We have a leader now,' he says, 'who's trying to bring all the black people in the world together so that they can work shoulder-to-shoulder with one another to gain their rights. Mad Garvey[1] is his name and no one knows who he is or where he came from.'

'I don't know,' I says, 'whether you'd welcome a white man like myself to your cause? The way I can help you is that my skin is whiter than that of most white men. On top of that, I belong to a race of people who've suffered seven hundred years of war, famine and oppression for the sake of freedom until we finally achieved it – or until we were close to getting it anyway. We identify strongly with others that are oppressed or treated very badly. Surely you've heard tell of the Irish, the race of people who are fighters everywhere they go, the race who've suffered more injustice than any other people in Europe have ever done?'

'Of course we've heard of you,' he says, 'and if you like, I'll bring you along to a meeting where black men from all over the world will be in attendance.'

'I'd be delighted to go to it,' I says.

He left and the next day I visited the library to find some books on the history of black people. I spent a fortnight reading them and the history of how they were treated was so terrible that I was ashamed to be a white man; and I had to admit that the injustice we suffered in my own country was as nothing compared to theirs. When the Spaniards and other nationalities left Europe for the New World, there weren't enough of them to take over and work the vast expanses of land they found there. The Native American people wouldn't work for them. They saw the white men as their enemy and they fought very bravely against the colonizers and this is a war that is barely finished yet. The Europeans got around this problem of the native peoples another way however. One day in 1600, a ship docked on the African coast and they massacred many of the locals and took many others prisoner and brought them to the Americas where they sold them as slaves. The black people hadn't done anything wrong. They were just earning their living the same as anyone else. They weren't hostile or wild. The people of Africa did their share of the work that the human race has undertaken; one industry that many of them worked in throughout the world was mining. And if they'd been wild or uncivilized they wouldn't have been much use to the people in the New World, would they? Their only crime was that they were black and they were deemed foreign. That, and the fact that people didn't know anything about them and that they were a different people.

This slave trade went on for the next few hundred years so that thousands and millions of black people were transported across the ocean and sold as slaves in the New World. They were all crowded into the belly of these ships and large numbers of people died on the journey. Those who survived weren't much better off. All that lay ahead of them was endless work and torture and being sold and traded, and treated like dirt. The black people under British control were given their freedom a hundred years ago and in parts of the United States they were freed nearly ninety years later. But even if they were technically free they often weren't free in truth. At least it was finally acknowledged that they were human beings rather than brutes or animals. They won't have any true freedom until they turn against the white race however and before it's all over the white people may well regret how they have treated them.

One of the most incredible aspects of this history is what happened in the West Indies where it was proven that the blacks were as resourceful and efficient as any of the people buying and selling them. The island of Haiti was under the control of the French until the developments of 1789. There was a man on the island at this time by the name of Toussaint L'Ouverture. He organized all the slaves into a fighting force and defeated one of Napoleon's marshals and took the island back from the French again. This was one of the biggest achievements of all time. L'Ouverture's successor was a man named Jean Christophe,[2] the man known as the Black Napoleon. No man who's ever lived had the reputation for power and violence that he had. He expected the French to return someday to try and re-take the island and was constantly preparing for this possibility. In order to be ready for the French, he built a massive fort 4000-feet high, a fort that can still be seen today on the highest hill of the island;

this fort will still be standing in a thousand years from now, given that its stone-work is as strong and stable as the great pyramids that the Egyptian kings built – structures that continue to amaze the world. There are still thee hundred big guns positioned on the walls of the fort to this day.

Many unusual stories have done the rounds as to how Christophe built this fort. Some people say that he killed all the stonemasons that worked on the project once the fort was completed. They say that he normally executed prisoners by throwing them from the ramparts and down into a gorge that was 1000-feet deep. They say that one day he visited the site to see how the work was going and saw a hundred men struggling with a giant rock that they were trying to push uphill and place inside the fort. They couldn't get this rock to budge however.

'Kill one in every four of the men,' he told his guards 'and they'll push it up to the top.' They killed twenty-five men but those who remained couldn't get the rock to budge.

'Kill twenty-five more of them,' Christophe ordered. 'Fifty men will push the rock uphill.'

Another twenty-five men were executed and the fifty who were left succeeded in forcing the rock uphill.

When Napoleon was beaten and sent to St Helena, Christophe hated him – for the simple fact that he was still alive following the rebellion. He often said that if he himself was ever vanquished, he wouldn't have had the audacity to go on living after such a terrible humiliation. And sure enough – the man was as good as word. When he grew older, he fell sick. He tried to kill off the infection using alcohol and managed to hold the illness at bay for a while. But he was resting one day when word reached him that the people had turned against him and that they were destroying his wheat-fields at the foot of the castle. Christophe grabbed a pistol and killed himself.

It may well be that many of the stories told about him aren't true but there's no denying that he was as incredible a man as ever lived. I spent a lot of time thinking about the West Indies after hearing his story. I could see that black people would contribute greatly to world progress, if they were only given the freedom to do so. If I ever managed to become king of the West Indies, I would really shake up the world, I thought. Maybe I'd even return to Ireland someday surrounded by a coterie of black bodyguards and take over my native country and maybe I'd talk some sense into the people there?

I went to the meeting that Matthews had told me about. There were men of every colour there – from men who were as black as coal to those who were bronze-coloured as autumn leaves, men from Africa and from Australia – and from all the islands of the Atlantic and the Pacific. I spoke to the meeting and praised their ancestors; I described their kings now asleep beneath the Egyptian pyramids; I recalled their bravery in Abyssinia and the incredible deeds of Cetauaio in South Africa. I reminded them of Toussaint L'Ouverture and the Black Napoleon. I told the meeting that they had ances-tors as powerful and as incredible as any group of people in the world. I asked them to unite and to drive the white man back to the colder northern countries he'd inherited as his right. They listened in amazement to me and I sensed that night that they might easily have made a king of me, if I'd wanted them to. We organized a consultative council for the next meeting. I was the head of this council and Matthews its secretary. We had ten other members whose job it was to act as spokespeople for the various different black nationalities and groups. I said that we'd need a ship and two hundred men as officers, and that we'd need money to keep us going for a month or so. We decided to raise the money in and around Cardiff as soon as possible and that we'd have another meeting the following week. I went home that night and I was on a high. It was as if I was walking through mist on a mountain peak. My own road was guiding me to a new country of nature and sun, the likes of which has never been seen before by most of us on this side of the world. My imagination ran wild – like the powerful waves that build and crash loudly on the birth of the storm.

I had a dream that night that I've never forgotten. I was at the top of a nameless mountain on the peak of which stood a great tree. The tree was torn from the ground and its roots lay above the branches. This tree was related to me. My inner being was within that tree and I knew that my whole life was entwined with it from the very beginning of time and right up to that very moment. And a terrible sadness came over me to see that tree torn from its native soil and its roots so badly destroyed. I have always remembered that dream ever since and it is not easy to hold onto certain dreams. But our night visions frequently just mirror what has come to us during the day, a small moment of insight or perception – just as the sun lights up the clouds on a day of rain or the way a rainbow is formed. There was nothing prophetic about this dream of mine however because I never did go to the West Indies in the end. And even if we were at it every day since, we'd never have collected enough money to pay the passage of even one person across the ocean to the West Indies. I wandered the city streets the same as the others but I never did find anyone who yearned to contribute to the coffers of the White King of Black Men.

12

Over the centuries, the poets have often described how the mind stirs itself and blossoms again once winter has passed and the natural world renews itself and the birds are singing. This transformation is expressed in one of Raftery's[1] songs:

Anois, teacht an earraigh, beidh an lá'dul 'un síneadh,
'S thar éis na Féil' Bríde ardóchad mo sheol.

Now that Spring is here, and the days – they grow longer,
Once Saint Bridget's Feast has passed, I will hit the road.

I felt myself getting restless once Saint Patrick's Day came around and I'd been living in the same place for five months – from the previous November onwards.

I had achieved very little in that time – just sitting there in my room with a book in hand or ambling waywardly through the city streets. I was a rudderless boat lost on the tide, the wind buffeting me this way and that. I was alone and poor and cut off from the world. Life was passing me by and I felt like a stone left by the wayside engulfed by grass and weeds. I had to do something to escape this lethargy. After a week or two considering my circumstances, I finally acted.

One day in April I turned out my pockets and found I'd two pounds and ninepence on me. This was all I had left of six guineas that a newspaper had paid me for various essays I'd written previously. And I had no idea under the sun where my next money was going to come from or how I could avoid at least three months' hardship or more. At least I had enough money to return to Ireland, I thought. I had no interest in returning to Ireland however. In truth, I was sick and tired of the country and I knew going back there now would have done nothing for me either mentally or physically.

But what in God's name could anyone do with two pounds? If you could spend it on something you'd never forget, that might be different. Say, I happened to meet a prince from the East there and then and he was dying of the hunger, and I gave him a loan and he granted me hospitality and the sovereignty of ancient and foreign lands as recompense – now that would be a different story! But there wasn't a hope in hell something that magical and incredible might happen in in a dusty coal harbour the likes of where I'd found myself!

It came to me then that I should make my way through this country, out through its glens just as they'd done in the era of the Fianna, sleeping in places that once hosted warriors and heroes and meeting people who spent their days circling their small circuit of their houses – then leaving them again with a sense of wonder in their hearts in order to follow my own road once more. Not to find myself tied down again to any one patch of ground, or any table or bed. At least, such a trek could make one feel alive once more. I asked myself how far two pounds would bring me and guessed that it'd probably last me for as long as it took Muircheartach na gCochall Craiceann[2] to make his way around Ireland. Two pounds might take me as far as Scotland where I could see Sciath Ailín overhanging Loch Rannoch and the russet mountain plain back west to the glens where the tribes of Uisneach had once found themselves on foreign soil. I'd always had a fondness for Scotland, a country whose story is intimately linked with that of Ireland. Some Scottish heroes are recalled in the folklore of Donegal and I'd seen a book once that said – whether rightly or not – that it was from Scotland that the Mac Grianna family had first originated – that they were of Scandinavian blood and had migrated across to Ireland in the time of the Gallowglasses. I'll walk to Scotland, I said to myself.

I went out then to buy weapons and clothes for the journey. I got a small bag, a ground-sheet, and a hat and trousers for the rain. Passing down the road and along by the shore, I remembered that a knife might prove useful and I checked in every shop window until I found what I was looking for. I read the name above the door. It was a foreign name – Lambadarios – a Greek, probably! I said to myself, and walked in. The man behind the counter was middle-aged and he had a friendly and intelligent air about him.

'I'd like to buy a knife,' I says, and he brought over two different types to show me.

'I prefer this one,' I says. 'It's closer to a sword.'

He stared at me in bewilderment before asking:

'I hope you don't mind me asking – but are you Greek?'

'I am,' I says. 'It was your name over the door that brought me in. It's not every day that you buy a sword from a man whose roots are in the ancient culture and nation that is Greece. I'm embarking on a journey out into the hills and glens and I'll be sleeping outside beneath the sky. And I'll need to have protection from any enemies and so that that I can quarter the spoils of the hunt come evening.'

I left Lambadarios staring after me in amazement. I'd have chatted to him about Greece for longer except that I was focussed entirely on the journey ahead. The knife cost me fourteenpence. I brought it everywhere with me for the next year and it'll be mentioned in my will. By the time I was ready for the road, all I had left was one pound, fifteen. I knew that this was probably nowhere near enough to keep me fed for a fortnight and that I'd have to find free lodgings wherever I went. When younger, I'd spent harsh nights out on the Donegal hills but I'd never slept outdoors an entire night except once in a haystack in County Limerick and that was a frosty night to boot. I was as well completing this journey in as manly a way as possible however. I stood up and made three vows:

The first one, that I wouldn't sleep in any house on the course of the journey.

The second one, that I wouldn't set foot in any car or train along the way.

The third one, that I wouldn't shirk any difficulty, or retreat from any challenge or struggle that came my way.

On the ninth of April, a Monday, I set off on my journey. I'd planned on setting off at dawn but between this and that, I was delayed and it was after one o'clock in the afternoon by the time I left.

I walked down Main Street and took the main road leading north. Once I'd walked about two miles, I found myself outside the city. I passed a pub called The Oak Tree at a fork in the road. There were two roads here, both leading northwards and I took the one veering left. It was a lovely day, cool but sunny, and I went on my way like a man setting out into the world for the first time, my step so light and quick. I wasn't long walking when I came across my first wanderer of the roads. He was pale and drawn looking with the makings of a small beard. He was carrying a little bag the same as me, and had a stick in his hand. But it was his style of walking that interested me most. He was only doing half the work that I was doing and I took note of his footsteps – so light that he barely touched the ground. Each step of mine was heavy in comparison and my soles struck the ground hard, but you'd have sworn this man was swimming on the soles of his feet, his footsteps were that light. I looked at him and he looked at me and his eyes said it as clear as day:

'What sort of a fool walks like that?'

I went on my way, proud of the strength in my limbs, but at the back of my mind, I was thinking that I'd be better off adopting this tramp's style of walking instead.

The main road led downhill and into the first glen with the river known as the Taff on my left-hand side and on either side were hills, trees and woods. The walking went nicely until it started to rain and I put my waterproof hat and trousers on as quickly as I could. It bucketed down for an hour or so and by the time it cleared up I was in the middle of the glen and the trees were shimmering and beautiful on the high hillsides above the river and the railway bridge that cut across ahead of me and disappeared with the tail of the rising hill, high and narrow as if into the sky.

I was in good form again until a tack in my shoe started pinching me and I stopped next to a big hole where some rocks had been removed, and took off my shoe. As I was messing with it, two men and a woman appeared from the back of a rise and made for the main road. They were tinkers. I soon found the embers of the fire they'd rested beside and I fixed my shoe. They disappeared along the road and I didn't see them again. I passed through five or six very small villages until I was about ten miles from Cardiff and I didn't stop for a rest at any stage along the way. I wasn't tired at all and it didn't even cross my mind to have a rest. If I'd known what lay ahead, I'd have taken it a bit easier. And then, I got my first view of the road ahead. I saw the way the glen narrowed and the houses all crowded in on top of one another inside it. I was at the mouth of the Rhondda. A few minutes later and a big, tall chimney revealed itself and I got the smell of smoke.

I already knew what a coal town smells like – like a section of hell that's been forgotten, the air thick with dust and smoke and ashes so that it quickly stings your eyes, and the houses more grim looking than anything you've ever seen – the faces of the people who live there excepted. If you want to know what a coal town is like put your nose to a fire that's still smouldering until the smoke begins to choke you and then take a tiny piece of ash and rub it between your fingers until you can almost taste it between your teeth. I knew all this and yet I didn't really understand the Rhondda. That said, I thought Pontypridd was a nice place – sat there at dusk between the hills, the church clock-tower at its centre. It was far more spacious and beautiful than the mouth of the glen. After I'd passed through it however, the roads became more narrower and more congested again. The glen itself was fairly expansive and had been widened by a railway track and a single street of houses but that was it. Every now and then a rocky incline appeared and the road rose sharply for a quarter of a mile or so. The mountains here were 1000-feet high or around that, and there were a few ugly man-made hills here and there formed by enormous dirty piles of debris removed from the mines underground. The occasional view of the river told you that the water there was as black as coal. I also spotted what looked like mills of some description with big furnaces inside them and great black machines that came between me and the light – there seemed to be very little work going on in them however. Next came a long series of small, low-sized houses divided by tiny narrow streets, every house the same. There was little sign of life or activity and it was quite dark between the streets as well. I still had fifteen miles to walk before I'd left the Rhondda

Valley again. After I'd been walking for an hour and there seemed no end to the road either, I felt hungry and went to look for something to eat – but I had some search for food I can tell you! I went into some very small, dark shops that had no provisions at all for sale and I think it was in the third one that I found some bread. I couldn't buy cheese or milk or eggs – for love or money. The poverty and hardship here was worse than anything I could have imagined; and it was worse than being out in the mountains also because at least you could feel free up high in the hills whereas you were hemmed in here. I continued on my way, along this dark, grim road that looked like it would go on forever.

TONYPANDY: This town appeared as if out of nowhere, a bright, happy-looking place in the middle of nowhere. There were plenty of shops there and plenty of light and the kids were laughing and playing on the streets. I went into a shop and bought two eggs and a piece of cheese, then crossed over to one of those cafés the Italians have where I ordered a glass of milk. I sat at the table, took out my knife, cut the tops off the eggs and swallowed them raw, then started on the bread, cheese and the milk.

There were three or four young lads from the village in having the crack, the same as other lads their age back in any Irish village would do. Their accents reminded me of a Belfast accent except that it wasn't as strong. They were lively and talkative but I wasn't in the mood for a chat. The seven miles of dark road had got me so down that I preferred not to talk to anyone. They looked like nice, friendly people and I preferred them to the people in Cardiff. But I couldn't make conversation with anyone all the same. One lad was sitting at the counter and glancing over at me fairly often. He gave me a good long stare. I didn't look like your average worker with short trousers and light tan shoes, I suppose. I had a small bag with me and I was eating my food the same as any man who'd gone through life and seen both the rough and the smooth.

'Looking for work?' he said quietly after a while. There must be twenty places where it'd be easier to find work than there in the Rhondda, I thought to myself.

My feet felt tired at this stage and I got great relief stretching them out beneath the table. After a quarter of an hour or so, I got up and went on my way again. It was getting late and some big damned towns lay ahead of me down through the glens and I'd sworn that I wouldn't sleep in any house along the way. I kept going and emerged into the countryside outside of Tonypandy. A road circled the hillside where the young people were out walking and playing and having fun. A shortcut led down between the houses and I followed this instead however – next came towns and more towns and trams on the streets. The glens were getting busier. Two hours later and I was thinking that it couldn't have been far off midnight and the road ahead led on into the distance as far as the eye could see – even if I had no idea how much further it continued on for. I have to reach the mountain somehow, I says to myself. Otherwise, I'll have broken my promise on the very first day of the journey.

I had a good look around. The hills were situated to the rear of some houses and I couldn't see any way of reaching them without getting around past the houses first. A short while later however, the glen widened out and I found a small street on the right-hand side and I left the main road and followed a lane to the back of a group of houses. No one paid any heed to me as I went around the back even if I was only a few yards away from their kitchen and they'd have got a surprise if they'd spotted me.

Some fields lay between me and the hill but the night was pitch-black at this stage and I could barely see anything. I felt my way along through the darkness and managed to reach a gate and opened it. I'm away now, I says. I hadn't gone more than five yards when I found myself obstructed by a wire fence however. If it hadn't been so dark and if I hadn't just walked a full twenty-four miles that day, I would have got through those fences somehow. But I sensed it was better not to take them on as well, at this point. I circuited the field but I couldn't find a gate or a gap anywhere so I went round it a second time. The light from the kitchen of one of the houses was barely nine or ten yards away and I was afraid that someone might see me. Eventually I retraced my route again and searched around for a while until I found another gate. I went up a small lane and I thought I was away with it again, but I'd only gone ten yards when I came up against another gate. I couldn't open this gate, despite my best efforts, and I climbed onto it. But I knew from the way it bent under me that it wouldn't hold my weight. I could have broken this gate into smithereens within a couple of seconds but I was afraid that someone in the houses might hear me and so I retreated a few feet and then tried the fence in a few different places – but I'd no luck on this front either. I was adamant that nothing was going to stop me reaching that hill but in the end I had no choice but to turn back.

I broke into another field. This one was wider but it was just after being ploughed and my shoes filled up with clay and muck. Not that I minded much. I found a gate and opened it and then another gate and I went far enough away so that I'd put distance between myself and the houses – so much so that even if a fifty-foot wall had appeared in front of me, I wasn't for turning. But just as I reached the other side of the field I came across a fence, the wires of which were more twisted and difficult than anything I'd passed through already. I messed around with them for a while and soon discovered that they weren't as complicated as I'd first thought however. It was the type of fencing that's made of metal cables spliced together at the ends and with wires twisting across and through one another like a fishing net. I felt around until I found the top of one of the wires and managed to loosen it and work it out of the mesh – and then I worked the cable in and out until I had four or five yards of it loosened.

Next, I threw my small bag over the fence and shoved my head and shoulders through the mesh and then worked the rest of my body through – for a moment, I was stuck halfway with the top half of my body on one side and my feet flailing and wriggling in the air on the other like a trapped fish. I finally forced myself down onto the ground on the other side and pulled my legs through however, then grabbed hold of my bag and climbed up along the side of the hill. It felt as if getting through those few old fields took more out of me than the entire journey that day and my entire body was bathed in sweat. I could tell by the way this fencing was made that it was designed to keep the sheep on the hill from breaking into the fields below – and it would have taken one powerful sheep altogether to have forced its way through it. I made for a hollow close to the peak of the hill where I pulled out my wet-sheet and spread it on the ground. I took off my shoes and changed my socks, and made my bag into a pillow. The wet-sheet was six-foot long altogether and five-foot wide and I thought it would do the job. Once I'd wrapped it under me and around me however, I found out that the five foot wasn't enough so I had to scrunch myself down into it and make myself smaller to keep the rain off my shoulders. I'm someone who usually likes his comforts and so I'd taken a blanket with me when leaving the last lodgings I'd stayed in and so I put this blanket beneath the wet-sheet to keep a bit of heat in my body. After the long walk that day, there was no way I could suffer too much hardship or cold that night.

But the ground beneath me was as hard as a rock and I could feel stones poking into my ribs. I couldn't sleep at all and I was shivering with the cold. Despite this, I fell into a kind of a daze. I heard bells in the town down below, the sound of trams I suppose, but all it put me in mind of was a poem I'd read years ago at school:

> *Hark! The faint bells of the sunken city*
> *Peal once more their wonted evening chime ...*

I remembered that it was James Mangan,[3] the poor man, who'd composed this poem and my imagination was alive, and I spent a long while discussing the poet in a low voice. I don't know who I was talking to in reality – maybe the enchanted creatures of the hill or some people I'd met long ago and barely remembered anymore. And when I was finished, I opened my two eyes and witnessed a terrifying sky and the darkness tearing the heart out of it. Eventually, I fell asleep even if I find it hard to believe that I really slept. I certainly didn't sleep like someone in a nice, comfortable bed with a roof over their head. I slept like a rocky crag that has always lived out beneath the elements. I slept without rest. I slept the same uneasy sleep that fingers sleep when the nails grow in them. And I wasn't long asleep when it rained and I felt the heavy drops on my wet-sheet, just half an inch from my skin. I didn't wake up as I normally would either. Shortly before dawn I felt restless, as if someone had suddenly thrown me outside beneath the elements. I shut my eyes again in an effort to resist the feeling of darkness and despair that engulfed me and I kept them shut until the morning cleared and the light appeared wan and pale on the faraway sky. I discovered a small hill opposite me formed by the debris of the coalmines and grown over with years of vegetation. I got up and I felt worse than I had when I first went to sleep. I gathered my things together and set out across the hill.

13

I crossed the brow of the hill just as the dawn fog lifted itself from the mountain with the morning, then went downhill in search of water. It wasn't too long before I came across some pipes that were servicing the town, and a short while later again, I came to a river. I washed my face in the water and took out my bread and cheese and ate my breakfast, then washed it all down with a big drink of water. I really enjoyed the food. The mountain water was ice-cold and the bread and cheese were frozen. The cold went through me in the morning now the same as the night before. I felt it in my body, right in the marrow. It was like the fish swimming in the mountain pool or the plant growing in the wilderness. And yet there was a purity and sweetness about that cold and I felt contented in myself. There was a joy in that river, I thought, and no wonder human beings had worshipped rivers since the beginning of time.

I got up and made my way across the hill and if I did, it wasn't without a struggle. Walking in the hills can be tough going at the best of times and my legs were still sore from the previous day. I reached the edge of the glen where a railway line cut through the landscape, a series of train-tracks covered in rust. I cleared the back of a hill and arrived at the foot of another. Over the way from me, I could see the houses of the Rhondda once more, and I was sure I had five miles of hill walked by then. I kept going in an easterly direction as I was hoping to avoid the grimiest towns if possible. Once I'd gone another two miles I came to a place with railway tracks and old trucks and iron cables lying around. I went down the slope and came to the railway line where a man was piling a bunch of support posts and placing them in one of these buggies or trucks. He looked over at me and said, nice and friendly:

'How are you?'

'Long life to you,' I says. 'You're an Irishman, and surely, I must have left the big towns behind me now.'

I hadn't however. I went out onto the main road again and passed a school and a church. Then I went down the street where the women were standing in the doorways chatting. It was almost midday.

ABERDARE: A nice, clean, lively and settled-looking place by the looks of it with plenty of people out on the streets. I passed a statue in the middle of the town – some man who'd won a prize for playing music in London. I can't remember his name now. I liked this about the place. The town was faithful to its traditions as Wales is a big country for music.

I went off to find something to eat. I'd sworn to myself that I'd try and live off raw eggs and cheese and the odd tin of salmon for the duration of my walk. But I was tempted now to go into a café and sit down and relax in comfort. I've always loved sitting in cafés and if I'd a book with me, all the sweeter. I entered a café where a dark-skinned, swarthy lad was serving – the exact same type of fellow as you'd often get back in Ireland – one of those placid, easy-going lads. He took a quick glance at my bag and shook his head. I think he noticed a tired look about me. He came over to the table.

'A ham sandwich,' I says, 'and a glass of milk.'

'Hot or cold milk?' he says.

'Hot,' I says, my mouth watering.

'I see that you're walking the country,' he says. 'I do a lot of walking myself. Have you come far today?'

'From Cardiff,' I says.

'Surely to God, you didn't come all the way from Cardiff today?'

'I nearly did,' I says.

'There's fine walking country around here,' he says, bringing over a map and pointing to it. 'Hold on now. This here is Aberdare. And here are the mountains of Brycheiniog.'

'That's the way I'm headed,' I says.

'There's a huge glen out that way. It is twenty-three miles from here to Aberhonddu, on the other side of the mountains. That there is the highest peak in the Brecon Beacons, at 3000-feet high. I climbed to the top of it once and there was a magnificent view out over the whole countryside from there. Out from Aberhonddu to Builth and to Rhayader and right around to near Plynlimon. Do you see that lake there? That's the place mentioned in the book The House Under the Water,[1] if you've ever read it.'

'I read it only last year,' I says, remembering the landlord who got tired of working the land and sold his estate to the city of Birmingham only for his ancestral home to be flooded by the waterworks.

'That's the place alright. There's so much to see back west. There's nothing much down south. The Rhondda's too grim.'

'It mightn't be beautiful but it's an amazing sight all the same,' I says. 'But I'd always prefer two miles in the hills than a mile on the street.'

'But surely you're not going to make Aberhonddu today?' he says.

'I'll try my best to make it,' I says.

It was about one o'clock when I left the town. I walked the four and a half miles to Hirwaen, the last town in the coal-fields. I was in a hurry as the more lonely glens were waiting for me in the latter part of the day and I didn't bother delaying to buy any food. But when I reached Penderyn, a village with a post office and a couple of shops, I sensed that I was on the edge of the wilderness, and I went into a shop there. A sturdy, easy-going-looking man was behind the counter and I heard him saying to his wife who was in the kitchen:

'Pump ar hugain wedi tri.' (Twenty-five past three.) I wasn't expecting to hear Welsh this close to the coal towns and my spirits rose.

'Prynhawn da,' I says. (Good afternoon.)

We chatted for a short while – for as long as my small bit of Welsh could carry me. I bought a tin of salmon from him and left. As far as I can remember, I walked a mile or a mile and a half until I reached a crossroads. On the road-sign, it said it was seventen miles to Aberhonddu from there. I was entering hill-country again and I had enough road walked since morning. I'd been walking in the hills from when I first awoke that morning until midday. Between climbing up and down hills, I reckoned I'd walked about eight miles in the morning and another seven from midday onwards. I was rightly exhausted at this stage – after walking twenty-four miles the day before – and with just the one break, and sleeping outside, and not getting enough sleep either and I wasn't eating enough to keep me going. I sat down at the crossroads and my legs from the knees down were worn out, and my heart was heavy because exhaustion destroys whatever joy is in you. My one advantage at this stage was that I didn't know what lay ahead of me.

A car passed me at the crossroads and a young girl came out asking the way to Hirwaen, and she was the last person I met until I was on the other side of the mountains. I kept going. It's not easy to describe ten miles of mountain without sight nor sign of anyone or anything, not a house nor a tilled field on any side. I've been to the base of Errigal and Barnesmore Gap but Brycheiniog Gap was as wide and long as any of them. The heat of the day had disappeared at this stage even if April heat is treacherous at the best of times. A cold blast of wind whipped up through the glen and went right into my bones – like river-water running through the rocks.

I'd never before felt (and hopefully never will) such exhaustion and pain as I felt that day in my two feet. My heart was telling me to stop and fighting me every step of the way, and it was only my will that overcame my body and kept me going. Because the will knew that the second day is always the real battle and if I didn't complete the twenty-four miles on this – the second day – I was a beaten man. I kept telling myself that I'd make it as far as Aberhonddu – another mile or two over the thirty miles even if I sensed deep down that those last few miles would kill me more than all the previous twenty-four miles had done. Eventually, I felt the urge to eat something but there wasn't sight nor sound of water and I had to walk on another mile before I found a stream. I opened the tin of fish and mixed it with the bread and drank some water. The bread was only a few thin slices but I knew now that I was right at the heart of the glen. And the cold and the pain and the exhaustion didn't really affect me properly until I sat down to eat. That's when I really felt it. I was sure that I'd never be able to get to my feet again. I was really struggling at this stage – as bad as I've ever been – and I don't know how I managed to pull myself together and continue on.

I went on my way anyway and if I was doing a mile and a half an hour, that was the best of it. I passed the Cardiff waterworks and a thought as strange as people entered my mind – that if this water-source failed, then the whole of Cardiff would be left destitute and similarly, if my body let me down now – my two legs felt like they'd been crushed between two heavy tombstones – I'd be finished too. The harsh thought came to me that it might be a week before they found my body, and even then there would be no big fuss about it. I stared straight ahead up at the incline of the next hill, as I made my way along the road – a beautiful view for someone who hadn't a care in the world, but all I could see right then was exhaustion and pain. Night began to fall and the first thing that came to me was that it wasn't falling half quickly enough. Because the smooth, grassy field between two houses is the loneliest place on earth once darkness falls and the light disappears.

Once or twice, after night fell, I passed a kind of a small caravan or cabin on wheels, like what the knights of the road might have used but I think it was the workmen who mend roads that had left them behind. They were open and I thought about going into one. It was threatening rain and I'd have had shelter there. I was put off by the thought of the hard floor inside however and I promised myself that I'd have a bed in a haystack somewhere that night – even if I'd to keep walking until the sun rose again. I wasn't sure either whether I had my twenty-four miles done and I was adamant that I wasn't giving in until I had this distance covered. And then, suddenly, on an impulse, I felt a new energy come into me as if the powerful expanse and hardship of the mountains had broadened my vision. I kept walking – and although I can't say that 'the Great Fool was quicker on his knees' than six other men were running, I can say that the Great Fool was as tough and determined as anyone from his two knees upwards. It began to rain.

I felt sure that I had passed through most of the glen by then and then I spotted a light a good way off in the distance.

It was far away from me and I knew I'd be in a right mess if that light disappeared before I managed to reach it. The night was black as pitch at this stage, so dark that I couldn't even see my own fingers or poke myself in the eye. I struck out for that light but it was as if it fled from my approach – like a being from the otherworld that meant me harm. I walked on another two miles but the light still seemed very far away and closer to where I'd been when I'd set out in the first place. A short while later, I came to a gate and a boreen leading into the woods. I thought that this boreen would bring me to that house with the light and I went on and passed through the gate. I walked for nearly a mile but there was no sign of a house or a shed or anything. I lost sight of the light and returned again to the gate.

By the time I got back to the gate, sheets of rain were falling so I went in under a tree and took out my waterproof hat and arranged the wet-sheet around me and lay down on the ground. People normally shelter under a tree whenever a shower of rain falls but believe me, if the rain lasts for a long time, then beneath a tree is the worst shelter of all – especially when the leaves are soaked through. It rained from dusk to dawn that night and I lay awake beneath it all the while. I don't think I slept at all but my mind was so tired that I'm not actually sure. I was so mentally tired that I couldn't think of anything – and the only image that came into my mind was that of a bear on its hind legs, swaying from side to side like a drunken man. When I tried taking deep breaths and settling down to sleep I started to shiver all over and my breathing became very quick and I thought I was having a heart attack.

I wasn't. It was just a shortness of breath because of the hardship I'd put myself through that day. It was difficult to lie down comfortably so that the blanket covered me properly and I had to get up at one stage and rearrange my bed. I stretched out my legs anyway and even if I'm not sure that I didn't sleep – I can't say for certain that I was awake all the time either. Maybe I slept the entire time except for the part of me that was conscious of the heavy rain and my bones tormented with pain and exhaustion.

When the day cleared, I got up and I felt happy and grateful just to be back on my feet again. My wet-sheet was soaked although she'd kept the rain off me. I went out onto the main road and two hundred yards down, I spotted the sweetest-looking haystack any knight of the road has ever seen. Another quarter of an hour and I could have slept there the previous night. I was nearly four and a half miles from Aberhonddu and between the hills I'd climbed since morning and the main road and the distance I'd covered through the woods, I made out that I'd walked at least twenty-six miles since the previous day. I had won the battle. That said, those first two days really destroyed me, especially the way the toughest part of the journey had arrived at the end of the day and the fact that I'd only had the ditch for my bed. It had left a psychological scar that had diminished the joy of walking. I can still feel some of the exhaustion of that second day even as I sit here now comfortably writing about it this evening. I'll probably still feel it even many long years after tonight.

14

After walking for about half a mile I came to a café. If you ever go this route yourself you'll see it, Tyrhos, about four and a half miles outside of Aberhonddu. There was steam coming from the chimney and a young lad was outside watching over cattle at the back of the house. I asked him whether the people of the house were up. He told me they were and I went in. It was quarter past seven in the morning. I ordered some food. A side of bacon hung from the ceiling of the house and I got a slice of it. I had a good feed – the first meal worth talking about since leaving Cardiff. And I sat by the fire until it was after eight o'clock. No one made much in the way of conversation with me although the woman of the house asked me whether I was Scottish. I said no and told her that I was Irish. She said that a Scotsman was living in the area and that he loved being outdoors in all weathers.

'He's obviously very fond of any kind of healthy living he can get for free,' she said.

It was fine and dry as I walked to Aberhonddu but I'd only just passed through it when the rain started again. It lasted most of the afternoon. I didn't have much walking in me that day. I sat down quite often and once I even lay down on my back and stretched out on the side of the main road with my rain-hat and wet-pants on and the rain lashing down on top of me. I was trying to get used to lying beneath the rain and become immune to it. The countryside around about me was smooth and grassy on all sides, the first such land I'd come across on my journey. Nothing much happened on the road until I reached Llyswen, twelve miles from Aberhonddu. As I approached this town the cold and the gloom was really getting to me so that I went into the garden fronting a big house near the main road and lay down in the shelter there. I wasn't long there when I felt something in the air. I don't know what it was but the feeling of despair left me and a sense of joy coursed through me that I wouldn't have felt if I'd spent two hours resting somewhere else. I was so happy in myself that I pulled out my knife and carved the word 'Diolch' [Thanks] into a tree out of gratitude.

On the other side of Llyswen, I spotted a café and I said to myself – I'll have another good feed here for myself and to hell with the money. I went in and a short, kind-hearted woman – by the look of her – prepared me a big meal. She asked me whether I was staying the night but I told her I wasn't. Once I'd had enough to eat and rested for a while, I went over to the door and got ready to leave. But the rain was lashing down so heavily at this stage that it actually made me anxious. I went back in and said that I'd stay the night.

I had broken one of my vows now. I'd been out under the rain for two thirds of the time since beginning my journey however. I'd walked sixty-seven miles and spent two very rough nights lying outdoors in the hills. I might as well tell the truth. I was afraid that a third night outside in that weather would be the death of me.

Once I felt the soft sheets against my skin that night I knew it was the most valuable three and sixpence I'd ever spent. The soreness left my feet and I fell asleep within minutes when it would have taken me an hour or two outdoors. I slept for ten hours solid and when I woke up I felt human again.

When I left on the fourth day after a fine breakfast and a good night's sleep I felt a renewed energy in me even if my feet were still sore. A fine green glen lay ahead and round-topped hills rising up to six hundred feet on either side covered in trees. A big, wide river ran through the area and it was one of the most beautiful glens I'd seen in a long time. This was the only glen I've ever seen where there was poetry inscribed on the trees. At first, I thought that the bright timber signs attached to the trees were just boring old notices but once I came closer I saw that they had done something here that was perfect for a place of such incredible beauty. Because what more noble way to elevate poetry publicly than to inscribe it on a tree?

Here's one of those poems untranslated and exactly as I read it and I'll never forget its words:

Hail stranger, who when passing by
Halt in the precincts of Glanwye.
Know all, you've but a right of way
– None to despoil, or hunt or stray –
And, halting here, you owe a duty
Not to defile my Fishing's beauty,
With orange peel, and paper bags,
Remnants of food and filthy rags;
Or what is worse, by smashing bottles,
That have appeased your thirsting throttles.
Think of the cruel trap thus laid
For the tender flesh of some courting maid.
Burn what will burn, and what will not, keep
And dump on some distant rubbish heap.
Thus would I gladly make you free
Of what of right belongs to me,
Whilst for you all who do your duty,
Nature will smile with added beauty.

Never fear, I walked to Builth with little difficulty after reading verses such as this, I can tell you.

Builth was a nice, clean and orderly place but I didn't delay there because I wanted to achieve something that day.

'Which way to Rhayader?' I said to a group of men, standing on a corner.

'Rhayader!' they said, pronouncing it with an English-language intonation. This was Radnorshire and not a word of Welsh had been spoken here for a hundred years. 'Across the bridge.'

Nothing particularly interesting happened on the way to Rhayader. I was leaving the plains behind and heading into the hills once more. I remember passing through a nice, small place named Little Hollow. Come nightfall, I arrived in a small village with one or two shops where I bought milk and eggs. It was nine o'clock and the night was pitch-black on reaching Rhayader. I'd covered about twenty-five miles by then but all I did was give a quick glance at the signpost and continue on towards Llangurig.

Making my way out through the glen, it was incredibly dark. Initially, the hills were low on either side of me but after I'd walked a mile or two, they became far steeper. I'd never seen hills like this before. The lights disappeared and all I could see were the two massive slopes on either side of me reaching to the sky. The wind sharpened as if a storm was on the way. I would have loved to have seen a light at this stage even if I still had plenty of walking in me. For the first hour of walking, it wasn't my body that found it hard going but rather my mind. It wasn't loneliness exactly but more a terrible feeling of dread, as if these giant hills were pressing in on me and I was abandoned and defenceless in the darkness. I heard the sound of water flowing downhill. A small shower of rain fell but then it cleared again and I continued on my way in the hope that the hills surrounding me on all sides grew smaller. But these hills continued on for miles and miles – enormous heights standing between me the earth's light.

Eventually, I saw a few gates and fields and I was hopeful of seeing a light before long. A short while later and I came across a house and I said to myself that I'd bed down for the night in a haystack there. The family was asleep as I went in the gate of the field but next thing, a dog started barking close to the house and it made an awful racket. I could make out the outline of a hay-shed in the darkness but I was afraid that the dog might give me away. I came across a small bank of ferns there, even if it was nothing much in the way of shelter. This'll do, I thought. The fern-bank faced the sheltered side and the first thing I did was sit down and rest my back against it. I'd walked thirty miles altogether that day.

I got up after a while and took three or four piles of ferns from the bank and lay down again. It was nice and comfortable at first but after I'd been lying there for a while, I'd flattened the ferns into the soil and I knew that I hadn't gathered enough ferns for my bed. But between exhaustion and laziness I just couldn't get to my feet again to gather some more. About two hours later I fell asleep.

I was awake just before daybreak, right before the people of the house rose for the day. I'd slept for about four hours probably. I had no food at all on me and so I'd to walk the five miles to Llangurig to get something for breakfast.

Llangurig is a small place, rocky and hard, with a church bell-tower looking down over the village from a height. The village sits in a hollow where the bases of two hills separate from one another.

I reached the village just before eight o'clock and if you ever travel that route yourself and you go into the Fairy-Thimble Hotel you'll see the table in the corner near the hob where I sat down that morning – unless they've changed it since. I told the girl there that I'd walked a hundred miles since leaving Cardiff.

'We've often gone out walking,' she says. 'But it's hard going. We never went out for a walk that we didn't come back on the bus.'

'I'll walk another two hundred miles yet,' I says, 'and I've sworn to myself that I'm not coming back by bus.'

I left again and made my way out the glen making for the foot of Plynlimon. Plynlimon is as high as Errigal, but the hills at the foot of the mountain are smoother and covered with sedge; it's a mountain that doesn't put its good side out somehow. I suffered on my journey that day in a way that I hadn't suffered before. Up to this, the walking had hurt the small of my foot but now it was the soles of my feet that were really painful. Maybe it was the hard, new surface they'd put on the roads that caused this. But anyway the soles were more painful than the smalls of the feet. I tried to keep to the margins of the road as much as possible but I couldn't do this all the time and every step I took on the main road was like walking on nails or on broken glass. As I made my way around the foot of Plynlimon I would have given anything for a new set of soles – and this was after me vowing to climb right to the top of the mountain earlier that week.

If I remember rightly now, the name of the glen near the back end of Plynlimon was Castle Glen on the way into West Ceredigionshire. I got some food from a dark-haired, brown-eyed woman in a house just in off the road there, even if it wasn't much. I walked on, still feeling hungry and circuited the shoulder of the mountain. The surface of the hill was very smooth and I lay down for a while on the flat of my back and listened to the music of the wind as it whistled through the glen. Ceredigion is a sweet place and there is a beauty all its own in mountains that are 2000-feet high, the slopes of which are as smooth as the plain. I saw a sign on the side of the main road that read: George Borrow[1] Hotel. 'May you have a white bed in heaven, Big George!' I says. 'You made a journey once through this same country that wasn't so different from my own.' I came to a crossroads, on the other side of which was a village called Devil's Bridge, a place that's very well known. But I wasn't going that way. I walked on a bit further until a tack in my shoe began hurting me. I took off my shoe but I couldn't do anything about it as the tack causing the problem was on the insole of the shoe. I suffered in silence until I reached a small town named Gogman just as dusk fell and it began to rain. I asked for lodgings in a small, low-roofed house to the left-hand side of the road.

There were three people in the family, a married couple and their daughter. The woman was a bit wary of me initially – lots of people are wary of me – but she chatted to me after a while.

'What's the name of this place?' I says.

'Gogman,' she says.

'It's nice,' I says.

'I think so,' she says, 'for someone who's out walking through this countryside. I wasn't brought up here myself. I'm English. I'm from Kent originally.'

'You wouldn't expect to find the likes of yourself this far west?' I says.

'Yes. Both places are very different from one another. The fields are tiny around here,' she says.

'That's always the way in hilly country,' I says.

Her husband came in after a while. He was Welsh. He had a newspaper in his hand and sat down to read it. After a while he looked up from the paper and said:

'They say that there's too much drinking going on in the House of Parliament in London – as if there's any harm in having a drink!'

'True for you,' I says, 'and their business is all pretence and show anyway.' He told me he'd worked in the pits at one point in his life, but that he'd been out of work for a long time.

'You look healthier for having given it up,' I says. 'Mining coal is a harsh life. They say that it's as dangerous for the man working down the mines as it is for the soldiers in war.'

He told me that there wasn't much work available around the area and because I was stuck for something to say, I told him that there was fine land down by Glanwye and that there was a shortage of workers there – something that I wasn't sure about at all. As we talked, the woman of the house told me that her daughter had something wrong with her mentally, and that she was slow compared to others.

'They were trying to get me to put her into an institution but I'd never let her go like that.'

The sadness of life is everywhere, I said to myself.

I went to bed early that night and woke up at half past seven in the morning. The woman of the house charged me five shillings for a very small light supper and for the bed and breakfast. I thought that this was far too much. Maybe she took extra off me for the conversation, as this is a habit some business-people have these days, especially the English. It's not in the Irish nature to avoid conversation even if Irish people can be bad enough themselves when greed gets a hold on them.

15

I'd spent most of my money at this stage but at least I'd had a rest and plenty to eat and the morning was fine and the low hills of Ceredigion looked nice. I wasn't long on the road when the land levelled out a bit. A few miles from Aberystwyth, I came to a crossroads and took the road northwards. I had about four miles walked when I spotted three tramps up ahead. They were walking slowly and it didn't take me long to catch up with them. But a man, sitting on the side of the road, stopped them for a chat just as I approached. I walked on past them however, as I'm impulsive when irritated and I wasn't about to satisfy your man sitting there and be waylaid by him also. One of the beggars turned and gave me a glance as I passed by and if I've ever seen death in a man's eyes, I saw them in his in that moment. No one knows what haystack or ditch or poorhouse your body will be found lying in before this week is out, I thought to myself.

I passed through Capel Bangor, after which the terrain turned very hilly again. I met a hunt with riders and a pack of dogs and the dogs surrounded me, sniffing me. A dog can be a dangerous animal and I didn't know whether they might be circling me for the attack. The riders were standing to one side of the main road and the same thought may have gone through their minds also as they moved nine or ten feet away from me and the pack of hounds followed them.

TAL-Y-BONT: A nice town set between scrub and hills. The sun was shining brightly as I came into the village and walking up the street I heard the sweetest and most elegant Welsh I've ever heard. The dulcet-toned Connacht-man! I says to myself. The western part of every country must be the same.

About half a mile outside the village, I got a glimpse of the Irish Sea. There was a slope down below me and about two miles of low-lying land, half of which was marsh stretching out to the sea. I waved my hat in the air with delight, as I reckoned I had one third of my journey done by then – nearly a hundred miles through harsh mountains before reaching the sea again here up north.

I followed a beautiful route now, westwards along the shore and the mountains rising high inland. The colours of the countryside here were similar to Wicklow without a shadow of a doubt. Ireland is more like the southern parts of Europe, I think, as regards climate and the nature of the landscape – than is the island of Britain. This is how I'd describe it: the northern part of Ceredigion like Wicklow, Merionethshire similar to County Down, and Caernarvon similar to Donegal. I passed through tiny villages nestled beneath ancient bridges, and hilly peaks and brushwood overhead. And I promised myself that I'd return to Wales again one day when I was in a better way and spend more time there. I spotted a small village named Taliesin,[1] and it made me wonder whether there was any link between this village and the poet who's as renowned in Welsh eyes as Oisín is to ourselves in Ireland. It was Taliesin, they say, who made the following prophecy for the Welsh people:

That will come, a ravenous and black beast
Savagely over from Germany,
And it will crush Britain painfully
From the Severn as far as the North Sea.

And Britons will be left weak,
And hemmed in by the foreigners in every fort;
Their language will live and they will praise God,
But they will lose their lordship except for remote Wales.

But after the years of misery,
British triumph will come again;
And they will carry the sweet day of victory
The upper hand over crown and land.

Shortly after midday, I climbed in over the ditch off the main road and had something to eat. Once I felt full, I stretched myself out on the ground and smoked a cigarette. Who did I see coming up the road then but a tramp, one of the men I'd passed out earlier that morning, fourteen or fifteen miles back the road. He wasn't going at a ferocious pace by any means and it was difficult to believe that he'd caught up with me that quickly.

'You made good time,' I shouted over to him, 'unless you got a car some of the way?'

He hesitated momentarily as if unsure how to respond to this, then said:

'Not at all. I didn't get any car.'

'That amazes me,' I says, 'seeing as I passed you early this morning, and I'd have thought I was at least one mountain ahead of you at this stage.'

He stood there and waited for a minute as I swung the bag over my shoulder and the pair of us walked out the main road together.

He was a small man, low-sized and light, and something under forty years of age. He had a narrow, tanned face, lively, black eyes and sported a moustache. You'll see thousands of his type in the big cities of northern England. His rig-out and clothes were distinctive and suited his wandering life. He had long, black hair, an inch or an inch and a half of which jutted out at the back from beneath an old cap. He was carrying a fairly big, heavy bag on his back, wore two overcoats, and a pair of shoes, the tops of which had been cut away for comfort's sake and the heels of which were at least an inch and a half thick.

'You've seen a good bit of the country, I'd say?'

'I'm not long in this country here,' he says, 'but I've travelled the whole of England and Scotland. I'm from England myself, from Yorkshire.'

'It's not good there at the moment,' I says.

'It's not,' he says, 'not since the war. Growing up, I worked in a saddler's but that fell apart after the war. I went to Scotland then and worked there until the Great Depression in 1923, when I was made redundant again. I vowed then never to do another's day's work again.'

'Walking the roads is a harsh life all the same,' I says.

'It is,' he says, 'especially in the winter. But I don't do much walking in winter. I stay in poorhouses. And I don't sleep outdoors in winter either; I'm not sleeping outdoors yet this year. The human body can only take so much.'

'It's true for you,' I says, realizing that by walking my own road, I'd been a lot more courageous than I'd first imagined.

'Where do you go,' I says, 'when you sleep outside?'

'In haystacks,' he says.

'Do they ever give you any hassle about it?'

'They don't,' he says. 'As long as you don't do any damage, they aren't hard on you. I usually ask people for permission to sleep there beforehand.'

You're an Englishman through and through, even if you were one hundred years on the road, I said to myself.

I took out some cigarettes. I've always hated it when people make little of others or ignore them, no matter who they are and I offered him a cigarette.

'I don't smoke anymore,' he says. 'That's another habit I've overcome.'

'You did well beating that one. Smoking is nearly as bad as work.'

A few seconds later, I asked him:

'So, which of the three countries, Scotland, England, or Wales, do you like best?'

'You can't really generalize,' he says, truthfully. 'They're miserly enough in all of them.'

'The majority of the human race are miserly. They prefer that to honesty. Maybe it turns out cheaper for them in the long-run,' I replied.

As we were talking, we spotted another tramp on the road ahead of us. He stopped and waited for us to catch up with him. He was Welsh, a small, wiry fellow with ginger hair of the type you'd find anywhere in Ireland. The three of us walked on together and they accepted me as one of their own, and it's rare enough that this happens to me. Normally when I find myself amongst people who have the reputation for decency, they're cold and hostile towards me. It might be that the same people would describe me as a fine person to others; that said, anyone who got to know me so well that they fought with me would never say that. When I'm in a good mood, I haven't a care in the world. And I couldn't have asked for better company than these two men.

We weren't long walking when the conversation turned to the issue of Communism. The Englishman knew a fair bit about it but the Welshman didn't.

'It has to come at some stage,' says the Englishman. 'It came to Russia and it'll come in here too.'

'If it came in the way it's supposed to,' I says.

'I don't understand it at all,' says the Welshman.

'This is what I understand by it,' I said. 'Say, for example, that shop over there now ... instead of that shop being owned by one individual and that person always watching out in case anything is stolen from him – everyone would have the right to go in and do what they want with the goods on offer and take whatever they want from the shelves. People would only take what they needed and no more than that.'

'Humph!' says the Welshman, and I could tell by him he'd loved to have had the chance to try something like that.

'You wouldn't take any more than what you needed,' I says, 'because there'd be no one to give it to once you'd stolen it. Everyone would have enough to keep them going.'

This set him thinking, even if I knew in my heart that he'd steal something and pass it onto others, given half a chance. And I knew that if he didn't have anyone to share it with, he'd lose interest in stealing too. Ah! The truth, the truth! How few ever walk that road and how close it is to the surface of the things even in the most dishonest of men!

I tried to get a bit of chat out of the Englishman next.

'There are twenty million people too many in England,' I says to him, 'and what do you think should be done about it?'

'They won't do good by those people, you can be certain of that,' he says. 'I know what we should do with them. There are plenty of fine expanses of land out in Australia and Canada and they should send them out and set them up so that they can make a living out there.'

'That would be alright,' I says, 'if Canada and Australia wanted them, but they don't.'

'They don't,' he says, 'but they should say to them that they're either part of the Empire or they're out of it.'

The Empire still exists, I thought to myself.

'Anyway,' I says. 'I'm not sure that you could make good farmers out of city people and they're the ones who are out of work in England.'

'I can't see why not,' he says. 'They're strong enough and they're clever enough and working on the land can't be harder than any other kind of work.'

'They're strong enough,' I says, 'and they're clever enough but I'm afraid that agricultural work isn't as easy as all that however. Anyway, no government would do it, the way things are these days. They might send out a hundred thousand people a year at most. Before such emigration took place the workers would need to have control of the whole thing and they'd have to have a good leader.'

We changed the subject then and the two tramps discussed different aspects of their daily lives. They gave their views of different poorhouses and farms. Such-and-such a place was infested with vermin and such-and-such a place was too miserly. Eventually, the Englishman said that it was time for us to have a rest and we took a break from walking for a while. The other two grabbed hold of a rock and sat down on it. I have a habit of stretching myself out in the ground – but I could see that what they'd done made sense and so I picked up a rock and sat down also. It's easy to get a chill from the ground.

A mile or two further on, we came to Glandyfi.

'Do you see that pub over there?' says the Welshman. 'A man broke into it recently but he was caught. He wasn't patient enough and got drunk while he was still inside.'

'That was stupid of him,' I says, 'not to do his stealing first and have his drink later somewhere where he was safe from his enemies.'

The other men said this was true for me and the chat turned to thieving.

'It would be worth stealing a motor now,' says one man.

'It wouldn't be easy to steal one,' I says, 'as the authorities would have the number of the car and the name of the driver registered on paper forms now and they'd be able to track you down no matter where you went with it.'

They didn't look like they knew too much about this side of things.

We discussed twenty other types of thievery – from banks and post offices and the like – and I told them whatever I'd heard about it. We passed the time like this until we arrived in the village of Machynlleth.

'What's the name of this place?' says the Englishman.

'Machynlleth,' says the Welshman.

The Englishman tried to pronounce the name twice and the third time he said something that sounded close to it. I was able to pronounce it fairly easily. It sounds similar to 'Machunchleat' if you were to spell it in the Irish language.

'There are no large towns out this side,' says the Englishman, 'as there are down south. I think Cardiff is probably the biggest, the capital city.'

'It's the biggest city but I don't know whether it's the capital,' says the Welshman, surmising that the Welsh themselves wanted to make Aberystwyth their capital city.

'There was a time once and this here was the capital city of Wales,' I says pointing to Machynlleth and remembering that Owen Glendower[2] had once held his parliament there.

This really amazed the Englishman.

We went into Machynlleth passing a forge on the outskirts of the town.

'I know the blacksmith in there well,' says the Welshman.

The Englishman began to recite poetry:

> Under a spreading chestnut tree[3]
> The village smithy stands;
> The smith, a mighty man is he
> With large and sinewy hands.

'I see that you have a love of poetry,' I says. 'Maybe you've composed the odd quatrain yourself, have you?'

'I haven't,' he says. 'I was raised in a place where there was nothing but dirt and grime everywhere. Maybe I'd have composed poetry if I'd found myself in a place with the beauty of the world all around me when I was younger and if I'd got an education and learning.'

I walked with them into the middle of the town. Then, as I was leaving them I wished them well as follows:

'May your travels prove fruitful and may your curious minds never grow old and may you never tire of the beauty of this world. You both have a wealth that is hidden from many other men that might deem you poor. Never share that richness of yours without due acknowledgment of its value.'

I left them and they went off to look for the poorhouse and I went into a café. The house with this caf in it looked very like an Irish house, more so than any other such place I came across on my travels. That is to say that it was as Welsh a house in Wales as a house in Ireland is Irish. A picture of a young Lloyd George hung on the wall, one dating to before he had grown his hair long and it had turned grey. A framed testament also hung high on the wall stating that a particular man – the man of the house, I think – was a member of the order known as the Ancient Order of Druids. It reminded me of the old days when John Redmond's picture was in every second house in Ireland and there were green flags and Home Rule everywhere you went.

I was still indoors eating when I noticed a policeman checking cars that were passing the window outside. The policeman came into the café and made straight for the kitchen and I was on edge immediately. I have a second sense about the likes of this before it comes my way. I listened in on the conversation for a moment and heard the following:

'The majority of them don't have enough money to pay their way on the train even.'

And I says to myself, you're the same as most people these days, you are hasty and short-tempered. And by the souls of my ancestors and by the pride of the Irish nation, I'll smash your ribs if you hassle me. You're about the same size and even if you weren't … You saw me come into town with those two tramps and you said to yourself: 'I could take this man in a fight.' But you haven't tried yet.

You'll understand from this – the sort of things that the artist has to endure as they make their way through this world.

I left the town a half an hour later and continued on in a northerly direction. It was easy to tell that you were in the north now. While the hills were grassy and smooth down south, they were rougher here. I'd walked twenty miles since morning and it was another sixteen miles from there to Dolgelly and I didn't know if there was any house at all on the way. And it was another hour before the sun went down. I said to myself that I'd hit the road hard and do a powerful, manly blast of walking that day, whatever else happened.

I hadn't gone far when I met a man who chatted away to me nice and sociable. Many of the Welsh are friendly and will greet you warmly. We spent a while in conversation. He asked me where I was from and I told him that I was from Ireland.

'I've been to Ireland before,' he says. 'Over in County Limerick. It was fine land around there. And although there was fighting going on at the time, and I was told that it was dangerous, no one bothered me at all.'

'Of course, they didn't,' I says, 'and why would they either.'

'We've an Irishman as our parliamentary representative for this area also,' he added.

'You couldn't have a better man,' I says. 'A man who'll fight his corner for you and won't let anyone push him around.'

'You're right about that,' he says. 'I can't say anything bad about the Irish. I was working in the pits with some of them down south. There were men there from all over – even black men. And they were fine people also – quiet, easy-going men.

'As nice as you'd ever meet,' I says. 'It's brutal work down in the pits?'

'They gave me the toughest work of all,' he says. 'I was strong, that's why. You're a strong man yourself. Because I was strong it wasn't man's work they gave me but an animal's work, the work a horse might do.'

This man looked quite strong alright. I was an inch or two taller than him but we were around about the same weight. A big, strong fellow with an honest outlook on the world. I liked him.

After chatting for a while, I went on my way again, and the glen grew harsher looking. All around me, the light was disappearing and it made floods of rain. Night fell. The mountains grew higher. I came to a village named Corris and I'm not sure what it put me in mind of exactly. I went through the glen and passed down through the fearsome gap that leads to the foot of Cader Idris, blinded by rain all the way. It was so dark that I could see very little of the road in front of me. A bus passed me at one point and its lights lit up the glen on my left-hand side and I saw the huge drop that was in it.

It wasn't long before the road dipped and went downhill and I thought to myself that this was surely the mightiest hill I'd ever descended. Down and down I went, so that it was like I was descending to the very bottom of the world, and this on the worst night for weather since I'd first set out on my journey. I came to a crossroads eventually down in the glen and I saw that I was halfway there, and that it was another eight miles to Dolgelly. Twenty-eight miles in one day is enough, I says to myself, but O Lord, where'll I lay my head tonight in this terrifying glen here? Next moment, I spotted a light across in the distance from me at the foot of the mountain and I made for it. But I've never seen a light that was more difficult to reach than this one. There was no sign of any path at all and I got scratched and torn going up through ditches and fields. When I reached the far side of the field, I spotted a bridge beneath the light and realized why the light was there. It was there so that people could make their way across the river. Between fences and ditches made of tall scrub and bushes I couldn't reach the light and I had to turn back. I went further along the main road and came to a sign that said 'Path to Cader Idris.' I'm alright now, I thought to myself.

I followed this route and it brought me to another river crossing and another bridge. I grabbed hold of the railing on the bridge as the night was pitch-black and it would have been dark at the best of times in this enormous glen. I walked out about five or six feet but I couldn't feel any more railing after this. I froze and was left standing there like a statue. This bridge is broken, I thought. I could hear the powerful current of the river roaring beneath me and I'd no idea whether I was just one foot or fifty feet above the water or whether this river was six-inches or six-feet deep. Believe me, it was difficult to take that next step. But Mac Grianna took that step despite the total darkness and the fact that I was alone in the middle of nowhere and despite Cader Idris and the lashing rain and the exhaustion. The next thing I felt some small stones beneath my feet; half of the bridge was in bits.

I made my way up then through a copse of trees and I saw the light from a house across the way from me but before I'd reached that light I came across a small, empty, old house and went into it. The house was nearly a ruin. Pieces of the roof were still hanging on here and there and I found a corner where there was shelter. I went outside and gathered a bunch of ferns. There are ferns growing at the foot of Cader Idris that are more than four- or five-feet long. They were soaking wet but I didn't care as I had my wet-sheet with me.

This was the loneliest place that I slept in during the entire journey.

16

When I woke in the morning, the day was fine and sunny again, even if it was still fairly cold. I pulled myself together and went down to the main road again and soon I had my first good view of Cader Idris. It's only about a hundred feet higher than Slieve Donard Mountain but it's definitely twice as wide and it's rough and craggy and has white patches on its peak like snow. It is eight miles around the foot of the mountain to Dolgelley and at least twice that if you wanted to loop the entire mountain. It was one really fine-looking glen that morning as I made my way around the foot of the mountain, with the long, narrow lake at the bottom of it, and the sea stretching out between the clouds and the land further beyond. There are few landscapes in the south of the country that compare with those up north.

I walked uphill along a new-built road. The traces of old paths and roads were still visible along the margins, worn away by rain. I made my way out along a cold, bleak ridge and sat down at a stream and ate my breakfast of bread and cheese, and drank some water.

Sunday is always a fairly gloomy and miserable day on the other side of the water and I was afraid that I wouldn't find anywhere to buy food. I reached a house called The Cross Foxes and asked whether they had any cigarettes. I managed to get a few and after I'd walked a short distance along the main road, I went in by a riverbank and had a shave. I couldn't forget that it was Sunday and that someone should be clean-shaven on a Sunday.

DOLGELLEY: A barren, craggy-looking town, I thought, and I was halfway through it before I spotted the glass windows and the timber in the buildings there. I found a café open after I'd walked the length of the town. On leaving the town again, I passed a few people who were just out for a walk and they looked at me with pity. I was as lame as an empty sack by then, I'm sure. My legs were killing me and felt as if they were about to give up on me again. There was no milestone or signpost on the way to Bala and it's hard to believe how far the road seems when you have no milestones telling you the distance. It was chilly and come afternoon, the cold was piercing. The great mass of Yr Aran mountain was to the west of me and it looked bleak. My feet were more painful with every step I took. Eventually I thought that if I took off my shoes and dipped my feet in the river I might get some relief. The minute I put them into the

173

water, it was like sticking them into a ball of fire however – but after a short while, I got great relief from the pain and I began walking again.

I wasn't too far gone before my legs felt as sore as ever however. A motorbike passed me and tried to drive me off the road into the ditch. I bent down and picked up a stone and threw it at the driver. If I'd managed to hit him and smash him in the head, you wouldn't have blamed me much. It's not easy to hit a fellow on a motorbike when he's moving away from you though. If he'd come back after me, I'd have fought him, even if I felt I was ready to collapse with exhaustion; it's rare for the rude or ignorant man to hang around for the fight once he's started it however.

Meanwhile I was anxious with anticipation for my first sight of Lake Bala and it took a long time before it appeared. This is a famous lake and there's no other lake in the country, bar one, that's as large as it. I saw her eventually and her low green rise covered in trees on the near side, and the bleak hills on the far side. There was nothing incredibly beautiful about her, I thought. Anyway, by then I wasn't really in the mood for hanging around to take the view of her in properly as night was approaching and I'd already walked twenty-three miles. I had to let some people pass me by on the main road before I could find somewhere to bed down for the night. Eventually, I found a gate and followed the nice little laneway leading up from it. I slept in a fine hayshed that night – the first time I'd done so since my walk began – on a farm called Gwern Hefn about three miles from Bala.

I got up in the morning and went down to the edge of the lake and washed myself. I didn't want to go into the town until people were awake so I walked around for a while and reflected on how it was by this lake that the English poet wrote the Morte d'Arthur, a long poem that I recited aloud to myself. I went into Bala a little later but if I was to be hanged now, I can't remember the name of the pub I got my breakfast in. I do remember one thing however; there was a poet's chair in the hallway, one of those chairs they give out as prizes at the Eisteddfod literary festival. I sat down and said:

I announce to you, o poet, my coming to your house
And I praise your chair as the seat of the kings,
I bring one hundred and one blessings over from Ireland
To every man who did not yield to the customs of the
  Foreigners.

A small man appeared from the kitchen just then and he smiled at me.

'You don't mind me asking?' I says, 'but are you the poet that owns this noble chair?'

'Not me,' he said. He returned to the kitchen and came back with another man. 'This here is the poet.'

We saluted one another and I asked him about the chair.

'I won it at the Eisteddfod here seven years ago,' he says.

'I'd like to hear the poem,' I says.

He needed little encouragement and launched into the poem immediately, and recited at least twenty verses of it. I only understood bits of it but it raised my spirits and for a few short moments we left all the paltry concerns of this mortal life behind us. He asked me to say a poem in Irish then and I recited *Laoi Argain Mhic Ancair na Long*.[1] He asked me whether I'd written that poem and I told him that it was older poetry but that I could recite a poem I'd composed myself and I recited some quatrains from *Creach Chuinn Uí Dhomhnaill*.[2]

'You've a Welsh voice in your head,' he says.

'Well, I'm telling you now that you have an Irish voice in yours,' I says. 'And I'll tell them back in Ireland that I met a man here who was an exemplar of his tradition. I'll tell them that the bards still hold sway in Wales the same as in the era of the kings.'

Then I went out and walked down by the edge of the lake and took stock of my journey. I had walked 168 miles in a week. All I had left was ten shillings. I couldn't go to Scotland on that. The best thing I could do was to return to the lodgings I'd last stayed in, I said to myself. I was 150 miles from Cardiff and I knew that I couldn't afford to stay in any other houses or eat in any more cafs and all I'd get from now on was the poorest and cheapest of food and mountain-water to drink.

I skirted the top end of the lake and set out in a southerly direction. After I had walked another three or four miles I came to the most stunning valley I'd ever seen in that country. I couldn't say that I'd ever come across a valley more magnificent than this one anywhere in Ireland either and Ireland is a more beautiful country than Wales. I met a man on the way and he told me that the valley was called Hirnant in Welsh, meaning the 'long valley'. I climbed the brow of a hill and a wood full of trees and miles of wire fencing appeared in front of me. I knew that I was getting close to the lake that the people of Liverpool sourced their water from. I came within sight of the lake itself and two or three small houses that had an English look about them at the far end of it.

I lay down on the flat of my back at the base of a signpost where two roads broke off and circled the lake – I was tired. I'd only walked ten or eleven miles since morning but my feet were already so painful that I kept going for the remainder of the day only by sheer force of will. I was like that for the rest of the week – completely crocked soon after midday each day and just about dragging myself along until it came time for sleep. Even if I had the power to relive that walk again today, I wouldn't want to do so.

Someone had ploughed the land on a section of mountain across from me and they'd made a fine, grassy field out of it – as neatly laid out as a tablecloth and with sheep grazing on it. I noticed two sheep and two lambs alongside them. One of the lambs was so fat and well-fed, it was nearly overweight. It was feeding off both sheep whereas the other lamb was so thin and weak looking that it had difficulty standing up. Every time it hesitatingly approached either of the sheep, they kicked it away. This was the second terrible sadness that I saw on my journey.

Dear God, I thought, who's looking after that lamb? Or has it been ordained in this case that one lamb should have two mothers and that the other is left orphaned? Are those two sheep a reflection of the people with money? Do the rich make one another richer, and do the strong destroy the weak? I'm afraid that I probably over-did this comparison or train of thought, but anyway. It was about a year later before it occurred to me that maybe the two lambs were being weaned and that that one of them had got a good head-start on the other. I'm convinced anyway now that the thin lamb must have been worth enough to someone or other that they were looking out for the poor creature.

Still and all, this sight ruined the afternoon on me. As I walked the five miles down by the lakeside, it seemed to me that I hadn't felt as heavy-hearted and down in myself since I was in the Rhondda, even if the view here was incredibly beautiful – between water and trees, and high peaks on all sides. It was the most stunning view I'd ever seen.

I came to a bridge at the head of the lake and then a crossroads where I stopped a young lad on a bicycle and asked him the way. One road led towards England and the other went southwards through the area the Welsh call Trefaldwyn. I followed this road but I was soon unsure as to whether I was going the right way. According to the map, there was a road to my right that looked shorter than the normal way. As soon as I came to a right-hand turn, I thought I was probably going in the right direction but I'd covered three miles before I realized that this road only went a short distance into the mountains before it came to an end. I decided to make my bed in the first haystack I came across. I was lucky. It was the very last house in the glen. I figured that I'd walked nineteen miles that day but given how the signposts were arranged, I couldn't be sure.

17

When I got up in the morning I returned to the main road for Llanfyllin. Nothing much happened that day and it was just one step in front of the next, a hundred steps and then another hundred, a thousand steps and then another thousand – down south through Trefaldwyn. The early part of the day was fine but come afternoon, a big shower of rain fell. Still, I think that I probably walked twenty-seven and a half miles that day even if I don't know where the strength came from to manage it. I'd only had a little sleep and had slept outdoors on the night previous to that one also. But there's no understanding fully how the mind works; maybe the pity I'd felt for the lamb had done me some good in the end.

The following day I walked to Newtown in the morning and it lashed rain. I went into a shop to buy bread. There

179

were no loaves for sale in the shop but the woman behind the counter handed me one that had been sliced already and gave me the bread for nothing.

'You should go to the Guardians,' she said.

This was the first time on my road that I was considered a true beggar.

The weather was terrible that day. Everything was wet and I couldn't sit down or relax at all without putting my small bag and my wet-sheet down beneath me. I got tired and when I reached Abermule train station I went in and sat down in the shelter there. And then temptation came my way and I thought about taking the train. I had weighed myself and that didn't help. On leaving Cardiff I was fourteen stone exactly in very light clothes. I'd lost four or five pounds of winter flesh and I was probably about the right weight for me then. But here in Abermule, I weighed just thirteen stone, six pounds and this was wearing a big heavy coat that was wet through. I worked out that I'd lost a full stone in weight within just nine days. This was natural given the circumstances, I thought, but I'll kill myself if I keep on this way. I could feel the damp and exhaustion and loneliness I'd suffered in those nine days leaning down on me like a great weight and I got up from where I was sitting and read through the list of train fares. Then I copped onto myself and ran out of the station. Outside, I counted my money and found I'd six shillings left. That wouldn't have brought me a third of the way on the train. But if I'd stayed any longer in the station there, I'd definitely have taken the train, whether I'd had a ticket or not.

In the end I left the station and went on my way out the road again and if the words 'I went on' appear frequently in this story it's not without reason. I walked on at a nice, relaxed pace hoping to make Llanbadarn that night. I passed a small shed of a house on the edge of a bog and a ragged-looking man harrowing the field next to it. He was talking to another man who was passing on the road as I came along. I liked his manner and all the swearing and loud, dramatic talk out of him.

'There's nothing like the work,' I called over to him.

'By God, but this is bloody hard work,' he says. 'If there was any soil here, it'd be something but it's all heavy, sodden peat!'

'For the man who's brought up with it, it's no bother to him,' I says.

'By Christ, maybe it is no bother for the likes of him but I wasn't brought up with this at all. I'm from the Rhondda – from Bargoed. They're giving us out land to work these days and this is the type of land I was given. I took it, even if it's only as a pastime for myself in the end.'

'You're not working as hard as me so,' I says.

'By God, but aren't you just walking the road as a pastime for yourself? There's lots like you and they'd be worth a few shillings behind it all,' he says.

'You'd be surprised how scarce the shillings are these days,' I says.

'How far are you going?'

'To Llanbadarn first and then onto Cardiff.'

'If you're heading for Llanbadarn, there's a shortcut through the hills. Take the left-hand road up that way and you'll knock two miles off easily. There's a nice, decent woman in Llanbadarn (mentioning such-and-such a name) and she'll give you a good feed in no time. She likes her drop. You should call into her.'

I thanked him and walked on. The man had a cross-eyed, shifty look about him but I've often found his type more helpful than people whom others deemed kind or generous. People are afraid to be helpful these days.

I followed the shortcut anyway, but I'd advise anyone against ever taking the shortcut when you're in country that's unfamiliar to you. The road to the left didn't bring me to Llanbadarn at all. It brought me up to a house on the hill instead where a woman was living alone. She got a fright when she saw me and I barely got a word out of her, never mind any directions. I had to go cross-country through a lot of fields before I could get back onto the road for Llan-badarn. I came out onto an exposed ridge lashed by a violent wind; it was tough going with the savage wind piercing me to the bone. A young lad appeared on the road ahead of me, who was going home from school – even if it was nearly five o'clock in the evening.

'What kept you?' I says.

'They don't let us home till half past four.'

'What class are you in?'

'The seventh class.'

'Do you know any algebra at all?'

He gave me a confused look as if he didn't understand what I was saying.

'Where do you live?'

'That house over there on the top of the hill.'

'Is it far to Llanbardarn from here?'

'It's four miles sir.'

'I didn't think it was that far.'

'It's six and a half miles from our house to the woods,' he says. 'There's a ditch around the woods that's full of holes and our sheep are always breaking in there. And it's still a good, long way from there to Llanbadarn.'

I reached the woods and it crossed my mind that maybe I should sleep there for the night but then I thought back to that night in Brycheiniog Glen. I wasn't happy with how much ground I'd covered that day either – and so I went on for another mile. I spotted a house about fifty yards ahead. I'll go in there and have a rest, I said to myself. Walking closer, I tried to think of an excuse for the people to let me in for the night. A bollard blocked both sides of the avenue and as I lifted it out of the way, I saw that the whole place was overgrown. I bent down and went in under the bollard instead. There was no sign of poultry or pigs or a dog or anything, and the wheel-tracks in the earth looked old. The house was closed up and it looked as if no one had lived there for a long time and that no one was looking after the place either.

Here's my lodgings for the night, I says. I went to the door and tried it but it was locked tight and someone had placed a strong, new bolt on it that wouldn't break easily. The windows of the house were in fairly good condition and secured from the inside. I spent a few minutes thinking and decided that it'd be stupid of me to try and break into a house while it was still daylight – and so I walked away again.

But once I'd about a mile done on the main road I knew that I was still nowhere near Llanbadarn. And it also came to me that I could light a fire back in that empty house and have a nice, relaxing evening for myself there. I sat down and rested on the side of the hill for a short while, unsure of what to do. It's not easy for someone to retrace their steps back along the route they've just walked and you can't break into a house without keeping a close eye out all the time. Eventually, the thought of the fire made me return however. Dusk was falling when I reached the house and I went around the back and had a good look. There was a bank of earth about four- or five-feet high back there and a dirty ditch between that and the wall of the house. An old pile of wet hay stood on this bank further up from this and it had a fork sunk deeply into it; it looked as if nothing had been touched there in a long time – as if people had just abandoned the place suddenly right in the middle of their work – or as if they'd died or had been run out of there, or something.

I spotted something just then that raised my spirits however. I found a small window at the back of the house where the glass was loose and the only thing holding it in place was a piece of metal wire secured from the outside. I took out my knife and hacked the wire away from the nails. The glass came loose but it fell and broke before I had a chance to catch it. I threw my bag in through the window, then stuck my head through.

I was able to get my shoulders through – just about – and, after a struggle, I managed to squeeze the rest of my body through the window, twisting and turning until I was inside.

I found myself in a small room that looked like a washroom. The house had two other rooms. It had a fireplace and other fittings – so that it almost looked luxurious to the outlaw just in from the hills. It included a bucket and stool and twenty other things as well, so that I could have lived there if I'd wanted to.

The first thing I did was grab the bucket and go outside again to bring in some water. The mouth of the bucket was too wide however and so I had to bend it in at the sides to get it out through the window. Strangely enough, I never thought of opening the front windows of the house at all. I crossed the road to a river that was in the glen and returned with a bucket of water and squeezed it in through the back window again. I threw a few big forkfuls of old hay in through the window, then collected a pile of sticks and threw them in too. Then I climbed back in myself.

It was as dark as pitch inside the house by then and this made it a bit awkward bringing the hay and the sticks through to the kitchen. I arranged some hay and sticks in the fireplace, and set a match to it, but the hay was too damp and despite my best efforts it wouldn't light. To top it all off, I dropped my box of matches on the floor and I couldn't find it again. I ended up crawling around the floor on my hands and knees searching for it until I eventually found it again. Then I tore a page out of my notebook and managed to get the fire to light. I had enough wood in and soon had a nice fire going. I started to make my supper on my hunkers but between the heat and pure exhaustion, I kept nodding off, my head lolling between my knees. I made a bed out of the damp grass and slept as soundly as I've ever done since the day I was born and christened.

I don't know whether anyone noticed the light in the house at any stage after midnight that night or not. I don't know whether any wild stories about a ghost sighting between the river and the house did the rounds afterwards either. All I know is that when I left the house the next morning, I didn't see anyone on the road and I didn't meet a living soul as I made my way to Llanbadarn.

I felt renewed after sleeping properly for the night, so much so that new verses of poetry were coming to me thick and fast, and poetry only comes to someone when body and soul are in fine fettle. That's why poetry is as scarce in the world as it is today. Poetry blossoms in someone the same as the flower buds on the tree, it is the beauty that heralds the fruit. I was composing verses like the following one after another:

> *I came in from the mountains before sunrise*
> *Alone – other than Owen Glendower;*
> *Walking westwards through the glen*
> *Alone – other than the ghostly footsteps of long ago ...*

But I wasn't long forgetting these verses again as the rain appeared and April let me know that it was still shadowing me all the way. It cleared up around midday when I came to a small place called Llanbister and I bought a pot of freshly brewed tea and ate my bread with it.

As I approached Llandrindod, the day was fine and a there was a lovely sun in the sky. This town is very well known for its healing powers and I certainly felt that there was something special in the air there. I went into the town where I came across some big hotels and lodging houses, the biggest of which was the motor hotel – the motors get the best lodgings of all these days! I felt jealous and despondent in this town. I was nearly jealous of the motors themselves as I'd walked so many miles at this stage that I was nearly comparing myself to a motor. And the jealousy and despair revived the pain in my legs and they felt so bad that I thought I was going to die. I went into a park outside the town and sat down on a bench and I don't know how I found the strength to start walking again.

Around nine o'clock that night, I arrived into Builth and I knew I was back on the same road I'd walked when travelling northwards initially. I went out through Glanwye looking for a haystack. I thought I was grand but next thing, a man came out of a house carrying a light, and so I went on a bit further again. I walked four or five miles out of the glen into another field. There was a dog lying in the grass there and it growled at me initially but I made friends with it. He got up after a few minutes and left but by then we had a connection made and it was as clear as day that if he were human, you could say that he'd taken to me. I was happier in myself that night. I had walked a long way and I was within seventy miles of Cardiff and I sensed that the gift of walking was nearly mine.

18

Passing through the glen the following morning, the main thing on my mind was the fact that I was running out of money. I'd spent another sixpence on a pot of tea in Llyswen and all I'd left by then was one shilling and ninepence. I checked my map and saw that I'd have a job covering the rest of the way within two days but I had a shortcut ahead and a new part of the country to explore and I wouldn't need to retrace my route through the same places I'd walked before – so that was something.

I was delighted about the shortcut for two reasons. Firstly, there was an area ahead of me that was off the beaten track and as beautiful an area as I've ever seen. It was a landscape that was somewhere between rough and smooth, a terrain that wasn't overly level either. And everything about it was half-asleep. It was afternoon when I reached here but this was a place where it was forever afternoon, even in the morning itself. I came as far as a small town named Llangorse where a lake revealed herself to me through an opening in the hills. Lakes are scarce enough in Wales. After leaving Llangorse, I went out to Bwlch just as the cows were going home along the main road. I went in search of bread but there was nothing in the shops. I still had one piece left and I bought an egg and ate it raw. I felt lazy that night and as soon as it got dark I found a haystack to rest in. I could easily have walked another five miles but I didn't. This was the first time I'd felt lazy during the course of my walk. Come daybreak I was on my way again. I'd no food left at all and it was about five miles to Crickhowell. Walking along the road, I thought that maybe I could eat something that was growing in the nearby fields but all that was there was a field of kale. I pulled up a few plants and ate them until it started coming against me. It's not easy to eat kale, especially when it's green and raw.

Crickhowell is as nice a village as you've ever been in, and it comes upon you unexpectedly; it sits there in the foot-hills with that ancient look about it that gives it a special atmosphere. I went into a shop and bought a half a pint of milk and two and halfpence-worth of bread. I went up a side street and sat at the gable-end of an old house that had the look of a castle about it and ate the food. I enjoyed that time more than most during the course of the entire walk. It only takes something small to spark a poetic mood in someone and I thought to myself that here I was on the very edge of the world, sitting at the foot of an ancient castle in a place as remote I'd ever been. I didn't know what the castle or the hill opposite me was called and I didn't want to either. For all I knew, the Land of Everlasting Youth lay on the other side of the next mountain or hill or before I'd walked another mile of road – and I'd find myself back in the world I'd so often dreamed of when alone.

The human world and time don't tally however. Time would be the death of us only that we capture it and divide it into minutes and hours and that we do so many different things to delay its passing, things that appear foolish enough at times. I've never understood the logic of how we spend our lives. I got up and started walking and I left the joy behind me and faced into the hollow world of ruin instead. Even if you offered someone Heaven, they wouldn't take it, and this is as true of the most selfish man as it is of the most saintly. If you don't believe me, then start doing good for people and you won't be long finding out. We're so lacking in wisdom and intellect that the only thing that knocks us off our stride is the fear of death. You are no one else's friend and nobody is your friend.

I was thinking along these lines as I made my way up the main road and passed a poster-bill and stopped to read it. Anyone brought up in Ireland has a habit of reading announcements, whether a call to arms or a piece of propaganda, and that's why I paused to read this poster-bill. And this is what was written on it:

OF WORLD-WIDE FAME
The Prophecies
of
JOANNA SOUTHCOTT[1]

are proved undeniably true by their fulfilment.
She left a box of sealed writings over 100 years ago,
which was ordered to remain unopened until sent
for by twenty-four Bishops or clergy representatives
in a time of National Stress. It is prophesied in her
writings that England will not find peace until this
is done. It is then promised to be the first HAPPY,
ENLIGHTENED LAND to help the other nations.
Books and information (enclose stamp) can be
obtained from
THE SOUTHCOTT CENTRES

Who says that the English don't have faith and that they focus solely on worldly affairs I asked myself? In Ireland we thought that Colm Cille was the only one who made prophecies. And if Colm Cille's prophecy had been written on a billboard, I don't know how it might have appeared! Like the following maybe:

THE WORLD HAS HEARD TELL
of
THE PROPHECY OF COLM CILLE
Between scythe and sickle, the war will come.
On the seventeenth year Ireland will be thick with
blood. The eighteenth year, woe is me, where have
all the men gone? Every little stream will have
a whirlpool, every fool will have boots, and the
children will speak plenty of English etc., etc.
Books and information can be obtained from ...
(Enclose stamp)

But I could never imagine it happening – especially the bit about the stamp. I couldn't envisage Colm Cille's prophecies being recited anywhere except around a big turf fire in a place where everyone understood one another, and the mighty shadow of the hills outside and the powerful sea thrashed against the jagged rocks, and made its ancient journey to somewhere else, and the fierce loneliness of the world above the beds of the saints.

These images brought me another mile of road. The weather helped me also as it was a fine day until I reached the next town. I spotted a big mound of coal on the side of the road and a series of small, low houses and the sight of coal-dust and ashes brought it all back to me again. My heart sank like a fishing-line disappearing into the depths. I was going back into the Rhondda again. It was actually worse now that I knew the Rhondda lay ahead of me and I was returning there a bit more worn out than I'd been the first time.

Brynmawr was the name of this village and I had a choice of three routes from there to Cardiff. If it's right to call it a choice – because they were nearly all the same distance from my destination and they all involved passing through various large towns. I went on until I reached a village named Sirhowy and I gave the last thruppence ha'penny I'd left in the world for a loaf of bread. At the crossroads, I took the right-hand turn for Rhymney. As I passed through this village, I spotted a burly policeman on duty watching the cars passing. We glanced at one another but I continued on my way. I had the feeling that he'd try and stop me – don't ask me why. Next thing I heard a short whistle behind me. I ignored it, but then he shouted at me. He followed me for about ten yards before I came to a stop.

'Where are you going?' he says.

'Down the valley,' I says.

'What's your business there?' he says.

'Can't you see that I have two feet on me?' I says.

His eyes looked lifeless and drowsy one minute but they opened wide on hearing this, I can tell you.

'How far down the glen are you going?'

I glanced up at the sun.

'It depends on how long it takes. As far as Caerphilly maybe? You happy now?'

I went on my way. I hadn't a notion of going to Caerphilly that night but I thought it better to put him off the scent anyway.

The lack of places to stop and rest wasn't the biggest worry in the Rhondda but the fact that it was harder to find a place to sleep. This was the reason I stopped once I came into the first mile of open countryside – on the far side of Abertysswg, even if the day was still fine. I went up by the side of the hill and made a bed of ferns for myself and lay there watching as courting couples passed in and out onto the main road.

Night fell and the valleys filled with light. You'd have sworn that all the stars in the firmament had illuminated the Rhondda in that moment. I was filled with joy looking up at them and I was happy that I had only the one day's walking left, even if I was very tired by then.

The next day, I can't remember whether I had cheese for breakfast or whether it was just bread and water but I passed through the following villages one after another – New Tredegar, Pengam, Llanbradach and Caerphilly, until I was on the other side of the Rhondda again. There's a big slope on the southern side of this last village and I'd decided to eat the last bit of food I had left at the top of this slope. I was so keen to get to the top of the slope that it felt as if I'd never get there. People were out walking that Sunday afternoon, just as a pastime and there was me fighting every single step of the way and three hundred miles of hardship and hunger rooted in those two legs of mine, and I feeling every bit of it. Eventually, I made it to the top. I was familiar with this place already, the little wooden church that wasn't much bigger than a car on the edge of the road at the foot of the old castle and the park over on the left-hand side that I'd passed four weeks earlier. I went in over a fence and filled my bottle of water and ate every last crumb of bread I had left. Then I lay down flat on the ground and relaxed contentedly. It was only about five o'clock.

I got to my feet after a while and did the seven miles into Cardiff, my heart light and joyful. The roads skirting the city appeared in front of me like crabs' claws and I saw the mist above the bushes and the trees, and all of the chimneys and I noticed how paltry and insignificant the city seemed when compared to the great mountains beneath the expanse of sky.

My journey was over. I was proud of myself. If anyone had asked me why I'd undertaken my trek, I'd have had a job explaining it to them. It was my own way, this road of mine. It had strengthened my mind and toughened my body. I'd walked a long distance and it had proved difficult. But then there's no devil born that would have convinced me to do what was small or easy to achieve. I'd made a good beginning. Maybe someday I'd walk around the entire world. The journey had wiped away many of the foolish thoughts and worries that torment the person who suffers in their mind. Rather than being nervous and anxious afterwards, I was ready to tackle any of this world's hardships and difficulties. Another benefit of my journey is one that's not so easily put into words – those thoughts and dreams that revealed themselves and formed in my subconscious, the same as clouds appearing on the tip of the horizon. Such images might not reveal themselves immediately to me but they will surely come to me again someday when my boat is under full sail and I'm crossing the sea that has never been travelled. The entirety of the world lies on the other side of that small screen of words we cloak it with and they have a far greater power and meaning there than they will ever have here – where we now find ourselves – this world of routine and regulation where the blind lead the blind and no one knows what road to travel. I'd prefer to be considered odd than to be tied down. I'd prefer to walk the road in darkest night than to remain blind.

And so goes the story of my journey around Wales thus far.

19

I received some money from Ireland that brought me home again. I also managed to get free passage across the sea with a group of people that were attending the races on the Curragh. On the eighth day of summer, we made port in Leinster. This was the first time I noticed how much grass grows on Irish soil. There was as much grass on the margins of the railway line as there was in the fields of Britain – and as for the amount of land we let go to waste ... The day was fine as I made my way into Dublin and the Wicklow Hills were as inviting as ever.

But Ireland has one major flaw compared with other countries. It has a lethargy or what I would term a lack of feeling about it. You don't care about anyone else and no one else cares about you. And nowhere is this more apparent than in the city of Dublin. When I walked the Dublin streets, I always felt that no one was aware of my existence at all and I wasn't long back there again before I felt myself sinking into the darkest depths of my being once more. I visited the Grand Harbour to see whether the boat I'd taken the previous year, The Mermaid, was still there. She was still there alright – lying there as if abandoned in the same place as before. I thought of the song that Aodh Ó Dónaill, one of the Rannafast poets had composed, Aodh Mór, the man 'born subject to the fate that could never be fulfilled'. This was the subject of his poem:

The poet had a brother named Mánus, a man whom no one would have remembered if he'd belonged to any other family. He was a helpless little creature and once the last poet in the family had died – and only Pádraig and Mánus were left – had uttered the following to the gathering in the wake-house: 'Dear neighbours, don't you pity me today left with the likes of him as a brother!' They all thought that Mánus would never marry. He went around the place like a little old man with his hunchback, and yet he went out one night determined to get a woman for himself. Legend has it that his trousers fell off that night but that's a story for another day. A terrible night of wind followed the wedding and he imagined that the elements were angry with him and he was petrified. He began to make music about a boat that was swept away with the tide on a stormy night. And I ask any native Irish language speaker if there isn't the highest of poetry in this first verse:

*Is gasta mara sheol tú leat, a bháid mhóir, nuair a
chuala tú pósadh Mhánuis,
Trasna an Deán Mór 's anonn ar Ghaoth Dobhair
ag tarraingt ar bhord na Spáinne*

...

*How quickly you sailed away, o great boat, when
you heard of Mánus' marriage,
Across the Great Channel and past Gweedore, and
you making for the Spanish coast*

...

I began then and composed my own version as befitting
me and my adventures:

*Out from Great Harbour, you had the wind making for
the Spanish coast
No wonder you made the journey when you heard the
story?
And you left abandoned and treated as useless
And a dark-cowhide from back west in Móin Almhan
sewn into that hag's rig-out.*

After I'd been sitting there for a while staring out to sea,
I got up and returned to the city but I couldn't shift the sense
of anxiety that engulfed me.

I found it difficult to get lodgings. I was looking for the
cheapest one and I walked through most of the back streets
and the heat was a killer, and some of the lodgings-women
were unhappy with me and I was unhappy with them. Finally,

while I was in a shop one day drinking a glass of milk I asked the shopkeeper whether there were any lodgings on the street.

'There are two on this street,' he says. 'There's number thirteen but I wouldn't recommend that one to you. If you try number sixteen, that one's alright. Tell them I sent you.'

I went down to number sixteen. It looked grand from the outside, a two-storey house with a garden and a front gate. I knocked on the door and man appeared wearing just a trousers and vest. He was well built with a thick head of hair on him and looked more like a country person than someone from the city, and he was. I liked the look of him.

'Have you any room for rent here?' I says

'I do,' he says.

'The man in the shop below sent me up to you,' I says.

'Come in,' he says and we started talking.

'I'd say you've plenty of money, by the looks of you,' he says. 'I'd say you're educated and you've a good job too.'

'That's right,' I says. 'I have plenty of education and more and I write for the newspapers, and sometimes I've plenty of money and sometimes I'm short enough of it. I can pay my way though.'

I'd have been embarrassed to say I was rich – and to be looking for lodgings in such a run-down area.

'I have some money set aside myself,' the man says, 'I'm not working at the moment. I hurt my back and I'm looking for compensation for it. They're always asking me questions about it and I don't know whether it'd be better for me to go back to work or not.'

I couldn't work out whether this man was a clever buck or whether he was just plain stupid.

'Don't go back to work, whatever you do,' I says. 'The back is a tricky part of the body. If you go back to work now it might come against you later.'

'Do you think so now?' he says. 'Do you know much about these things?'

'That's just my opinion,' I says.

He brought me up to see the room. I know men who'd have struggled to lie down properly in it, the room was that small; there was just barely enough room for the bed in it. The walls were in a bad way. In fact, the whole house was a lot worse on the inside than it looked from the outside. I asked how much the rent was and he said six shillings. We made a deal for five shillings and I booked my room there.

'I've to go and get my bag now,' I says and left again.

When I returned the woman of the house was there and she asked me to come into the kitchen. She was a Dubliner from the slums, and I didn't like the look of her very much. The kitchen was filthy dirty and the house was wrecked looking from lack of care. When I went up to bed, there weren't enough sheets on the bed – just an old torn blanket that you wouldn't have thrown over a four-legged animal. I went down to the kitchen and asked for more bedclothes. They looked put-out at my request – especially the man – but they gave me the bedclothes anyway.

The following day, I went out to look for food. I found a street where I could buy a loaf of bread, a pound-weight for just three halfpennies. Another penny for a pint of buttermilk and I had my breakfast sorted. I bought the same again at midday and had another bite to eat come evening. I passed a week in this way. The weather was very good and I was out-doors during the day and anyone would have been jealous of me, I looked so healthy.

One day who did I spot coming towards me on the street but the blonde-haired girl, Macha Mongrua that I'd met over in Liverpool. She recognized me immediately and we chatted away for a good while until I told her I had to leave; I said to her that I was in a hurry even though I had nothing to do really. All she wanted to know then was where I was staying and I thought it was probably easier for me to tell her in the end. She called around two days later. She said that she'd been looking for me the previous day but that I wasn't in.

'For the love of God, what sort of a lodgings is this?' she says.

'Oh, there are some fairly important people staying here,' I says. 'We've a doctor and one or two others who weren't too badly off – at one stage of their lives anyway.'

'The boss-man here isn't right in the head,' she says.

'I wouldn't worry about him. He's cute enough in his own way.'

'He wouldn't let me in at all first,' she says, 'and he was right ignorant about it too.'

'He's looking for compensation money for some injuries he got at work,' I says, 'and I'm sure he thought that you were spying on him.'

'That must be it,' she says. 'He was suspicious of me in the beginning but then he brought me in and gave me tea.

He chatted away to me then for ages and the things he was coming out with! He was talking about you as well – "He comes in here and I don't know him from Adam. He might be John Dillinger[1] for all I know."'

I had a good laugh at this because it was around then that they were on the hunt for John Dillinger but no one could capture him. Anyone with an interest in daring and heroism remembers that buck who led the state police in America a merry dance that summer. I was proud that someone had compared me to him.

Things went alright until the following day. I was out all day and it was after eleven that night when I returned to the lodgings. I was ten days lodging there by then and I'd paid my first week's rent on my very first day there. And I planned on leaving the second week's rent until the last day of the week. The man of the house opened the door to me when I got back that night.

'If you'd been out much later we'd have been asleep,' he says crankily but I ignored him.

'That'd be a bad one now. Leaving me out on the street all night like that,' I says half-joking.

'You could call up to the guards and they'd let you in for the night,' was his gruff response.

His comment annoyed me even if I remembered his John Dillinger remark earlier so that I couldn't be too angry with him about it.

'Why? What've I done wrong this time?' I says.

'We don't keep anyone who doesn't pay his way,' he says.

'I don't owe you people anything,' I says.

'You do,' he says. 'You owe a week's rent.'

'I don't and while you're at it, you won't get another penny from me.'

'Get out of my house,' he says.

'I sure will and you're welcome to it,' I says, 'and you're that close to me smashing your head in for you as well.'

'You would in your arse ...' he says.

I was at the top of the stairs by then and he was retreating from me towards the kitchen door; he was all talk. I grabbed my bag and left, then set off for my brother's house. He was asleep but I hammered on the door and Séamus stuck his head out the window.

'Are you sure that this here isn't John Dillinger?' I says.

'I am,' he says.

'If you're that sure,' I says, 'come down here now and let me in, will you.'

I only stayed two or three days with him. There wasn't much in the way of conversation between us, just talk about football matches; the usual conversation that the Irishman who's married and settled down, and has neither won nor lost but is just getting on with life, goes on with. Séamus admitted to me that he hadn't read even one book in that previous year. And he advised me to get a job. I told him that if the poles on the road outside turned white that week, I'd get a job the next month. We had less and less to say to each other as the days went by. Even at the best times, we could never agree on anything – not even what way the wind was blowing. On my fourth day there, I upped and left.

I ran into two people that day whom I'd known for years

and who were involved in Irish-language issues, one of whom was a writer. One man worked in the civil service and the other man worked at something similar, I think. I couldn't make conversation with either of them however. I tried to tell them a story but once they saw that it had nothing to do with current affairs they weren't interested. One of them was carrying a bundle of exam papers under his arm and the sight of them nearly made me sick. I thought I'd seen the last of them thirteen years earlier. I left them there and went on my way again. They were hostile to me now. I had Irishmen and Englishmen now as enemies.

> *And that's it, O sweet and red-lipped one*
> *My sole fear by sea and by land*
> *Fionn and his Fianna in pursuit of me*
> *And I cornered and hungry in a narrow place.*

I found lodgings next with a widow who was as poor as myself and we put up with one another fine for the summer.

20

I left that lodgings at the end of the summer. I found a place with two rooms, one to sleep and to cook in, and the other for writing.

This house was as dirty a house as I'd ever been in. There were as many flies in the back room as there were in Egypt when Moses placed his curse upon them. I had the two upstairs rooms and the family lived on the ground floor – a man and his wife, and their two children. And the few times I stuck my head in the door to have a look, it seemed to me that I'd never seen human beings living in as dirty a hole as this ever before. They were a lazy shower from what I could make out. He worked as a cobbler and he might have made a go of his business if he'd had a good spouse. But she preferred relaxing and reading to cleaning the house. It's not for me to criticize people who read but there's reading and then there's reading in it ... and the stuff she read was absolute rubbish. And just because someone reads a good book doesn't mean they aren't well capable of being productive at the same time. This woman was like a lot of young ones these days; she was materialistic and had all the grand notions but that was as far as it went. There aren't many women these days who have much go in them, it seems to me. They can work in offices but let no one tell me that people in offices do real work. I'm too old now to fall for that one anymore! And there's nothing that annoys a man more than a lazy woman; because where I was born and raised the lazy woman would perish quicker than the fish on dry land. And bad and all as the women are, the men are worse again these days. All they do is mooch around waiting to see where someone dropped a halfpenny by accident. I didn't like this man any more than I liked his wife. We got on grand until I'd been there close on six or seven weeks.

The lack of light was the first bone of contention between us. It was the same meter for the rooms downstairs as it was for my room out front. They asked me to connect my light to its own separate meter but I told them that I'd just put a penny into their one every time I needed the light. And that's when the tussle started about who'd wrangle more money out of the other. I was kind to them – until I saw that they were playing games and that they were up to no good. Then I worked out a way that I could use their light most of time. I bought a candle and used this any time the meter wasn't on. As soon as they put a penny in the meter, I'd blow out the candle and switch on the other lights. Any night they'd put a penny into the meter late, I'd sit up until I'd used every last sliver of light – even if I'd to stay up till dawn. This wasn't a trick that any poetic man would be proud of but my advice to you is this: always get in first and take your chances when you get them. Because the less hassle they give you in the beginning, the bigger the bastards they turn out to be in the end. The crook always starts with the small things because he knows what the good man doesn't – that it's the small thing that always leads onto something bigger.

This cat-and-mouse game couldn't have continued for much longer however as the tension was reaching breaking point. One night the woman of the house told me that I had to leave and the following day I went out to look for another lodgings. To top off my bad luck however, I couldn't find a new lodgings anywhere that day and had no choice but return to the same place again that evening. The minute I came in the door, the woman was straight over to me and her husband a step or two behind her. And they were aggressive:

'You owe us a week's rent,' they says. I had my rent paid up till the day previous.

'Where I come from, there are seven days in a week,' I says. 'Now, back off or you'll be sorry.'

I let a roar out of me and they backed away from me and I went upstairs. The man left after a while and returned with a guard in tow but the guard couldn't sort it out either. The man of the house tried his damnedest to persuade me to leave the room but I was having none of it and ignored him. Ignorant people always play tricks like that. If he'd got me out of the room, I'd never have got back in again.

The guard left eventually and I locked the bedroom door and slept soundly for the rest of the night. When I got up in the morning I went to my room out front only to find the door locked tight. All my baggage was in the room and a manuscript that Ireland might have missed if it'd been lost. The man was gone out to work. I asked the lodgings-woman for the key but she said her husband had it. I let another roar out of me and told her she was dead if she didn't unlock the door immediately but she ran frightened out of the house. I think that she probably went off to get her husband. I smashed the door in and grabbed my bag and I haven't seen that pair since.

I found new lodgings in a fine big house with spacious rooms, a place that looked as if it had belonged to wealthy people at one time. I had a room there and access to the garden at the back where I regularly walked up and down, thinking of stories to write or reflecting on all the cruelty and hardship of this world.

I was only two days in that house when I met a man at the door that I'd never have expected to see in such a place. I'm not very familiar with their like but I knew for certain – even if he was only half in it I'd have known – that this man was one of the gentry. He looked like he was drunk. Not that I gave a tuppenny-damn about his wealth and status or the fact that he was gentry. It made no difference to me – if he'd turned out to be a bastard and got in my way, I'd have knocked him down with a powerful belt of my shoulder, the same as I'd have done with any man – that's if he'd wanted to take me on, which he didn't. Come flood, flame and violence however, I'm still a proper Irishman underneath it all and I will show a gentleman respect if he deserves it – no matter who he is. Because the man who fears a gentleman is the same boor that would injure a greyhound or mutilate a racehorse. And the boor who'd destroy a greyhound or racehorse is the same as the man who'd steal a sheet from a corpse. There's too much talk these days of the rights of the lowly man. The poor man was given his way for the past hundred years and he made a really bad job of it. And so I stood aside to let him get past me. But he stopped in front of me and asked:

'You couldn't lend me a few shillings, my good man?'

And if you think that he didn't get that few shillings, then you don't really know me.

That said, the woman of the house admonished me after he was gone.

'He was asking you for money, I notice,' she says. 'You shouldn't pay any attention to him. That's Lord Glennagrew. His father left him an inheritance to buy up half of Dublin and he drank it all. His wife was laid up with bone disease when the bailiffs came to evict them from their home and she had to be carried out of the house on a stretcher. She got some casual work in the city after that and for a while she was forced to go out to work on her crutches. He's not staying here in this lodgings at all. He just comes in to visit her and ask her for drink money. I had to order him out at midnight the other night, he had so much drink taken, and he slept on a park bench for the night. He's useless; you can't convince him to stop drinking. There's a curse on the family.

They had a holy well on their estate at one time and people used to visit it regularly and do the rounds. The lord saw the people going to the well one day and asked them what they were doing. They explained it to him. He owned a thorough-bred horse at the time and it went blind. "The waters that heal a human being should be able to heal a horse too," the lord says to himself and what did he do but bring the horse to the well. They say that he had bad luck after that and that the bad luck has followed his family and his family's family right down to the present day.'

'O my Dark Rosaleen, Do not sigh, do not weep,' I says. 'You are still the Isle of Saints.'

I counted whatever money I had and the next time the lord visited the lodgings I bought a bottle of whiskey. I called into his room and he opened the door hesitantly – and yet as proudly as if he was showing me into his very own castle.

'Greetings and Salutations to you O Lord Glennagrew,' I says by way of announcement. 'Don't think for a minute that I'm trying to take advantage of you for a bit of company like some other rogue might do. You are descended from lords but I am descended from kings. The roots of my people go back as far as Mánus Ó Dónaill who was King of Tyrconnell in the sixteenth century when the Connells ruled all of the toughest and most powerful tribes from Glenmore in Scotland right across to West Connacht.'

'That's demned interesting,' says Lord Glennagrew.

'I come to visit your castle,' I says, 'with an offering of wine as a symbol of my friendship and respect. Let us drink to the health of ancient nobility and the princes of today who find themselves scattered on the wind to the four corners of the earth. The lord gave me a great welcome and we sat down to drink the bottle. The conversation wasn't as free-flowing as I'd first hoped, but we warmed to one another gradually. I told him something about my adventures. I told him that I'd walked the country in the company of the knights of the road less than six months earlier and that mountain and glen had become as one in beauty once more – now that I'd spent the evening drinking with a lord. It came as little surprise to him that I'd been tramping the roads with beggars and wanderers. There were none nobler than the wanderers of the road and none less foolish either. The following day, we each went our own way to take care of whatever we had to take care of – even if that wasn't much – and neither of us marvelled to the other that our fate was thus. A week or two after this, the lord's wife left the lodgings. She had a row with the woman of the house I think. There was that – and the fact that I'd become friendly with the lord. Life is truly strange and filled with wonder, I thought to myself. I left the lodgings myself shortly after this. I find it difficult to settle in any one place longer than three months. Once I've been staying somewhere for three months or so, it crosses my mind that there's something else awaiting me in a different place. Sometimes I think that I'm always running in case my neighbours get to know too much about me and I become one of them. Other times, I think that the world has a secret hidden from me and I have to keep roaming the earth until I discover it. Other times again, I think that I'm Seanchán Toirpéist[1] wandering the world in search of the Táin Bó Cuailnge.[2] And all the while, I fear that I'll wake up some morning to find that I too have grown old – the same as Oisín who bent down to help his few followers that remained and help them lift the load only for his harness to break. And how often have I said to the last writers in the Irish language, 'Shame on you, you crowd of wimps! Don't you have it in you to bear this small burden yourselves for a while?' Just as I have borne it every time. Once it was *Dochartach Dhuibhleanna*; another time it was *Ar an Tráigh Fhoilimh*; once it was *Creach Chuinn Uí Dhomhnaill* and another time again it was *Séamus Mac Murchaidh*.[3]

And many's the time that this same terrifying image has appeared before my eyes – the harness breaking and me falling to earth and men finding me there on the ground and they with a grammar book or a basic course in composition in their hands.

But still, I don't think that they'll destroy me. They broke[4] but maybe he thought there was something worthwhile in them and showed them too much respect. At times, he may even have thought that they had it right. But even if they were right, I'd never admit it. They can do their worst, but I'll keep ploughing the furrow that lies ahead of me. I'll get the better of them someday and I've a feeling it won't take that much to defeat them in the end. I might be struggling but they are falling apart entirely. They may have convinced themselves that they're stronger than me but deep down, they know that this is just pretence. I'll see the fruits of my labour in my own time and my name will be on the lips of Irishmen and Scotsmen everywhere one day yet.

And anyone who asks me to whom I'm referring here – I'll tell them that it's to the dark side of my own soul. It is those casual friends of mine that I have in mind. It is the remnants of the Conference of Kilkenny, that part of Ireland that is both Gaelic and anglicized at one and the same time. Some of them are in the Gaelic League, some are Republicans, some are Communists and others are in Fianna Fáil; some of them are in Fine Gael and many others are in none of these groups.

Those who betrayed us, they did it because they hadn't an ounce of the victor's blood in their veins. They are the people who fought hard enough and bravely enough but who always fought for the lesser good. They're the ones who were full of fine talk and ignorance but whose own kin got the better of them, the ones whose own women got the better of them; they're the people whom the tumult and the radiance of the city overwhelmed and the gossip of old wans, and the Golden Calf.

They are the same people you meet everywhere you go but who are too afraid to look you in the face; and even if you did give them the stare, there'd be just a dull laugh out of them. They are the same people who gained common sense when they should have secured strength and power instead. And as for all the other people in Ulster and Leinster and Munster and Connacht, bless them all! If they lost, they didn't really lose and if they were victorious it did them no harm. They were always on my side and they always will be.

And my own road still stretches out forever ahead of me. This road of mine – it veers around by the gable-end of this house and disappears off between the trees and into the night and the March winds high above. And at this road's end lie mountains extending out till the end of the earth and the naval champion out in front that protects all living things and tears open the darkness from noon to dawn with his great sword of light.

The house I'm staying in at this very moment is one that Liam O'Flaherty[5] lived in at one time and the one where Pádraic Ó Conaire called in and made conversation on his last journey to Dublin where he died. I didn't know this until I had taken lodgings here. I don't know where this road of mine will lead me next but I do know that the wonders of the world will seek me out. The entire world is full of poetry for the man whose fate it is to understand it and this well will never run dry. And for as long as I still have breath in me, I will lead the Irish people to the source.

NOTES

I

1. An Gúm

Founded in 1925 as part of the Department of Education by Ernest Blythe, the then Minister for Finance in the Irish Free State, An Gúm was an Irish state publishing company tasked with the publication of Irish literature, especially educational and literary materials. An Gúm's principal remit was to ensure a supply of textbooks and general books that would be required to implement the policy of reviving the Irish language. Following the Belfast Agreement, the organization became part of Foras na Gaeilge. In its early decades, many of An Gúm's publications included translations of famous and contemporary English-language books such as Stoker's *Dracula*. There were also translations to Irish of other renowned European authors and Irish authors who wrote in English. In addition, An Gúm attempted to support the publication of Irish-language novelists, the two most renowned of whom were undoubtedly Galwayman Máirtín Ó Cadhain and Donegal novelist Seosamh Mac Grianna.

2. *An Phoblacht (The Republic)*

This was a weekly, and later monthly, newspaper published by Sinn Féin in Ireland. In early 2018 it moved to a magazine format while also encompassing an online platform. Its editorial stance is left wing and Irish Republican and in addition to articles covering the conflict and ceasefire in Northern Ireland, it also explores issues relating to politics and trade union activism across the island of Ireland as a whole.

3. *An Droma Mór (An Druma Mór: The Big Drum)*
A novel about internal rivalries and divisions amongst nationalists within a small rural community in the Donegal Gaeltacht. The 'Big Drum' of the title refers to a large drum that is taken out of storage and played once a year during the Saint Patrick's Day parade by a different young man from the locality. This drum is a motif running through the narrative, one that is hugely symbolic in terms of both a local 'rite of passage' but also as a nationalist symbol. *An Druma Mór* by Seosamh Mac Grianna was published by the Oifig an tSoláthair, Baile Átha Cliath (Dublin) in 1969.

4. Aileach
The Gaelic chiefs and kings of Aileach belonged to the Northern Uí Néill (O'Neills) and were based at the Grianán of Aileach (Grianán Ailigh), a hillfort on the peak of Greenan Mountain in modern-day Co. Donegal, Ireland. The restored fort stands in a commanding position at the base of the Inishowen peninsula overlooking Lough Swilly to the west and Lough Foyle to the east. Irish literature has it that by the twelfth century the Kingdom of Aileach was riven by division and had ceded territory to the invading Normans. Most of the original ringfort is said to have been destroyed by Muirchertach Ua Briain, King of Munster, in 1101. Substantial restoration work was carried out on the site in 1870 and nowadays the site is an Irish National Monument and a tourist attraction.

2

1. Carraig Dun
This may be a reference to ancient times where a Gaelic fort was abandoned suddenly by its occupants.

2. Cathal Mac Giolla Ghunna (Charles McElgun)

Cathal Buí Mac Giolla Ghunna (1680(?)–1756) is one of the four most prominent of the south Ulster and north Leinster poets in the seventeenth and eighteenth centuries, a group that also included Peadar Ó Doirnín, Art Mac Cumhaigh, and Séamas Dall Mac Cuarta. Mac Giolla Ghunna is believed to have been born in Fermanagh and tradition has it that he initially studied for the priesthood before adopting a career as a rake-poet and a writer of ballad-poetry for the impoverished Irish-speaking populace of the northern counties in the early eighteenth century. His poem-ballad 'An Bonnán Buí' ('The Yellow Bittern') is one of the best-known songs in Irish and is still widely sung today. A Gaelic poet who had a strong association with counties Fermanagh and Cavan, Mac Giolla Ghunna is buried in Donaghmoyne, Co. Monaghan.

3. Odhraín

Tradition has it that Odhrán/Odran/Oran was a friend of Saint Columba. Saint Odhrán's feast day is on 27th October. He is believed to have lived for over forty years around the Silvermines area of County Tipperary, where he is said to have built a fine church in 520. In 563 he was among the twelve who accompanied St Columba to the Scottish island of Iona, where he died and is buried.

4. Rif Mountains

The Rif or Riff (Berber: Arif, Arrif or Nekkor, Arabic) is a mountainous region in northern Morocco.

5. The Book of Invasions

Lebor Gabála Érenn, known in English as The Book of Invasions, is a collection of poems and prose narratives in Irish intended to be a history of Ireland and the Irish people from the creation of the world to the Middle Ages. There are a number of versions of this collection of myths, the earliest of which was compiled by an anonymous writer in the eleventh century. According to The Book of Invasions, Ireland was 'taken over' or 'settled' on six occasions by six different groups of people: the people of Cessair, the people of Partholón, the people of Nemed, the Fir Bolg, the Tuatha

Dé Danann, and finally, the Milesians. Tradition has it that the first four groups were wiped out or forced out of Ireland again while the fifth group, the Tuatha Dé Danann, represents Ireland's pagan gods. The final group, the Milesians, represents the Irish people or the people known as the Gaels.

6. Art Mac Cumhaidh (Art Mac Cumhaigh/Art MacCooey, c.1738–1773)
Recognized as one of the last of the great Gaelic poets, MacCooey is believed to have been born in the townland of Mounthill in Creggan, Co. Armagh. His family were small farmers and the poet worked as an agricultural labourer during his life. MacCooey was educated in a local hedge school and wrote praise-poetry for the O'Neills, then the most powerful Gaelic family in south Armagh. He also wrote laments for the destruction of Gaelic culture and the demise of the native Gaelic ruling class subsequent to the Cromwellian confiscations of the mid-1600s as well as politically inspired aislingí or vision poems – a literary genre that was rare in Ulster – where he imagined the restoration of the Gaelic nobles and their power again in Ireland. When Mac Grianna gives his 'pretend-address' as Úir-Chill an Chreagáin in *This Road of Mine*, he is referencing one of the more famous of these vision poems that begins '*Ag úr-chill an Chreagáin is é chodail mé aréir faoi bhrón*' ('At úr-chill an Chreagáin where my sleep last night was sorrow-filled'). This poem/song occupies an important place in traditional Ulster song repertoire down to the present day.

3

1. Redmond O'Hanlon
Count Redmond O'Hanlon (c.1640–1681) was a famous seventeenth-century Irish rapparee or outlaw. Similar to other Gaelic clan chiefs of this era in both Ireland and Scotland, Scotsman Rob Roy MacGregor being one example, O'Hanlon was essentially an 'outlaw-for-hire' who worked for the Anglo-Irish landlords and the Ulster Scots merchants of the northern counties. In return for payment or what would be termed 'protection money' today, O'Hanlon retrieved horses, livestock and other goods stolen by bandits and highwaymen from landlords and merchants who placed themselves under his protection. This 'protection money' was referred to as

'black rent' by the Protestant settler class and was used to support O'Hanlon's network of clansmen and their families.

2. Harun Al-Rashid

Harun al-Rashid (known as 'Aaron the Orthodox/Upright' or 'Aaron the Just' in the Arabic) was an Iraqi leader or ruler between the years 786 and 809 – the peak of the Islamic Golden Age. Baghdad began to flourish as a centre of culture, learning and trade during the era.

3. Bodach an Chóta Lachtna

'Eachtra Bhodaigh an Chóta Lachtna' or the 'Adventure of the Churl of the Grey Coat' is the title of an early-modern Irish (sixteenth-/seventeenth-century) Fenian tale. The bodach is a trickster figure and a male analogue of the cailleach ('hag, witch'). In the early-modern storytelling he was frequently associated with Manannán mac Lir, the god of the sea in Irish mythology and the ruler and guardian of the Otherworld. Irish poet James Clarence Mangan in 1840 published an adaptation of 'Eachtra Bhodaigh an Chóta Lachtna' as one of the first prose works of the Irish literary renaissance and Patrick Pearse published a retelling of the same tale in modern Irish in 1906.

4. Ceithearnach Caolriabhach Uí Dhónaill

This is the central character in a medieval 'romance' entitled *Ceithearnach Uí Dhomhnaill nó eachtra an Cheithearnaigh Chaoil-Riabhaigh do réir druinge* (*The Foot-Soldier O'Donnell or the Adventure of the Narrow-striped Foot-Soldier according to some ...*). Another trickster/landless soldier-type in Gaelic tradition, a figure that has been forgotten to a large extent and who – as with Robin Hood in England – may have been an amalgam of a number of outlaw/rapparee figures. This tale in Irish by an unknown author is believed to have been composed c.1733. It was compiled and edited by Irish-language scholar Énrí Ua Muirgheasa/Ó Muirgheasa (Henry Morris, 1874–1945) and published by Conradh na Gaeilge in Dublin almost two hundred years later, in 1912.

5. Fianna

Small, semi-independent warrior bands found in Irish mythology. They feature prominently in the *Fiannaíocht* literature – the stories of the Fenian Cycle – where they are led by the renowned warrior Fionn mac Cumhaill (Finn MacCool).

6. Argain Mhic Ancair na Long

Argain, son of Ship's Anchor's Crowd – a pirate gang, presumably.

7.'An Draighneán Donn' ('The Brownthorn Bush')

A traditional Irish love song about a man and a woman who fell for one another at the fair and spent the day courting under a brown-thorn bush.

8.'An Buinneán Buí' ('An Bonnán Buí': 'The Yellow Bittern')

A traditional Irish song. See Cathal Mac Giolla Ghunna.

6

1. Uisneach

The Hill of Uisneach or Ushnagh is a hill and ancient ceremonial site in Rathconrath, County Westmeath, Ireland. Geographically, Uisneach is located near the middle of Ireland, and in Irish mythology it was deemed the sacred and symbolic centre of the country. It was also considered the burial place for various mythical figures and a place of assembly, associated with the druids and the Celtic festival of Bealtaine.

2. CID

Criminal Investigation Department.

7

1. Glas Ghaibhleann (Glas Gaibhnenn)

A semi-mythological figure in Irish oral tradition, a highly prized and magnificent cow of bounty (fertility) whose inexhaustible supply of milk symbolized prosperity. The Glas Gaibhnenn is one of a range of beings in Irish mythology embodied in particular landscape features or bodies of water, including rivers named after them. After the cow was stolen by Balor and taken to Tory Island (off the Donegal coast), Cian retrieved him, and along the way fathered the hero Lug Lámfhota (Lámfada) 'of the long arm' – possibly for his skill with a spear or his ability as a ruler. Tales concerning the Glas Ghaibhleann are widespread in later Irish and Scottish Gaelic folklore.

2. Roscrea and Mount Melleray
Roscrea Abbey and Mount Melleray Abbey are both home to Catholic Cistercian monasteries where meditation and silence are central elements in their spirituality.

3. Parthalán (Partholón)
A character in medieval Irish Christian mythology and legend. In Gaelic storytelling tradition he is credited with leading a large group of followers to settle in Ireland and is therefore a figure often considered a likely character-creation of Christian writers. It may be that this Irish figure originated from 'Bartholomaeus' or 'Bartholomew' and was a character borrowed from the Christian pseudo-histories of Saint Isidore of Seville or Saint Jerome.

10

1. Macha Mongrua
In Gaelic mythology, Macha Mongrua was a Celtic queen, the daughter of the chief known as Aodh Ruadh (Red Hugh). Legend has it that she could out-run horses, even while pregnant. Her name is associated with important places in Gaelic (Celtic) culture including Emain Macha (Navan Fort), one of the great noble sites of pre-Christian Gaelic Ireland, and Ard Mhacha (Armagh).

11

1. 'Mad Garvey'
This is a reference to Marcus Garvey. Marcus Mosiah Garvey Jr (1887–1940) was a Jamaican political activist, publisher, journalist, entrepreneur,

and well-known orator. He was the founder and first President-General of the Universal Negro Improvement Association and African Communities League (more commonly known as UNIA) through which he declared himself Provisional President of Africa. An advocate of both black nationalism and Pan-Africanism, his ideas became known as Garveyism. He became involved in trade unionism and civil rights activism in his native Jamaica initially before later living briefly in Costa Rica, Panama, and the UK. He joined the National Club of Jamaica, the first overtly nationalist organization on the island and rapidly became its Assistant Secretary. The National Club's publication *Our Own*, a publication that shows a strange congruence with the Irish Sinn Féin ('We Ourselves'), drew many parallels with the racist and brutal treatment of black people during the imperial project implemented against other colonized peoples such as the Irish. Coincidentally, the fact that Garvey's surname is very common in Donegal would have drawn the Jamaican activist and Mac Grianna to one another anyway. Garvey lived in London between 1912 and 1914 at the height of the Home Rule debate, a period when Irish Nationalism was acquiring a new vibrancy and militancy. The fact that the question of Irish independence was a subject of much discussion amongst literary people and intellectuals at this point meant the Irish novelist and the Jamaican writer had much more in common than might be assumed initially.

Returning to Jamaica, he founded UNIA in 1914. Two years later, he moved to the US where he established a UNIA branch in New York City's Harlem district and promoted unity between Africans and the African diaspora while also campaigning for an end to European colonial rule across Africa. Garvey was a controversial figure. Many in the African diaspora regarded his views as dangerous and were very critical of his collaboration with white supremacists, and his prejudice against mixed-race people and Jews. He was highly regarded for his engendering of a sense of pride and self-worth among Africans and the African diaspora after centuries of poverty, discrimination, and colonialism. Garvey is considered a national icon in Jamaica, and his ideas exerted a profound influence on movements such as Rastafari, the Nation of Islam, and the Black Power Movement.

2. Jean Christophe

This is a reference to Henry Christophe (1767–1820) who was a key leader in the Haitian Revolution of 1791 and the only monarch of the Kingdom of Haiti. Christophe was a former slave of Bambara ethnicity in West Africa who rose to power in the ranks of the Haitian revolutionary military subsequent to the Slave Uprising of 1791, a revolt which resulted in Haiti gaining its independence from France in 1804.

12

1. Raftery

Antoine Ó Raifteirí (1779–1835), known in English as Raftery or Anthony Raftery) was one of the last renowned poets or 'wandering bards' in the Gaelic tradition whose memory and work survived into the modern era in the West of Ireland.

2. Muircheartach na gCochall Craiceann

Muirchertach mac Néill (died 943), known as Muirchertach of the Leather Cloaks (Old Irish: 'Muirchertach na Cochall Craicinn') belonged to the Cenél nEógain sept of the northern Uí Néill (O'Neills) and is said to have been a king of Aileach at one time.

3. James Mangan

James Clarence Mangan (1803–1849) – born James Mangan – was a renowned Irish poet. Mangan is frequently termed Ireland's first national poet and his work encompassed a range of multifaceted styles and traditions including Romanticism and Modernism. He proved a major influence on the Irish writers who came after him, James Joyce amongst them. Joyce published two essays on Mangan, one in 1902 and the second in 1907.

13

1. *The House Under the Water*

This was a novel by English writer Francis Brett Young published in 1932. One of Young's life's literary projects was a series of linked novels set in a loosely fictionalized version of the English West Midlands and Welsh Borders known as the Mercian novels. These works were inspired by the construction of Birmingham Corporation's Elan Valley Reservoirs between 1893 and 1904. *The House Under the Water* recounts the completion of this complex and amazing feat of engineering and describes the building of the Elan Valley dams and the pipeline that carried the waters of the Elan and Claerwen rivers from Radnorshire across the countryside to the storage reservoirs in Birmingham.

14

1. George Borrow

George Henry Borrow (1803–1881) was an English novelist and travel writer. His travel books were based on his own experiences travelling through Britain and Europe. He developed a close relationship with the Romani/Gypsy people and they figure prominently in his work. His best-known works incorporating Gypsy life and characters were *Lavengro* and *The Romany Rye*.

15

1. Taliesin

Taliesin (sixth century AD) was an early Brythonic poet of Sub-Roman Britain who is said to have sung at the courts of at least three Brythonic kings. His poetry has possibly survived in a famous book known as the *Book of Taliesin* (Welsh: *Llyfr Taliesin*), one of the most famous of all Middle Welsh manuscripts. While this book is from the first half of the fourteenth century, at least ten of the fifty-six poems it contains are taken to have originated well before the tenth century. Welsh scholar Ifor Williams identified eleven of the medieval poems ascribed to Taliesin as possibly originating as early as the sixth century, composed by a 'historical' Taliesin.

2. Owen Glendower

Owain ab Gruffydd, the lord of Glyndyfrdwy (c.1359–1415), or simply Owain Glyndŵr (anglicized to Owen Glendower), was a Welsh leader who led a fierce and long-running but ultimately unsuccessful war of independence with the aim of ending English rule in Wales during the late Middle Ages. He was the last native Welshman to hold the title *Tywysog Cymru* or Prince of Wales.

3. Under a spreading chestnut tree
The village smithy stands;
The smith, a mighty man is he
With large and sinewy hands.

These are the first four lines of the poem 'The Village Blacksmith' by Henry Wadsworth Longfellow (1807–1882), an American poet and educator. Written c.1840, the poem was published as part of the volume *Ballads and Other Poems* (1841).

16

1. *Laoi Argain Mhic Ancair na Long*
The Lay of Argain, son of Ship's Anchor's Crowd

2. *Creach Chuinn Uí Dhomhnaill*
The Ruin of Conn O'Donnell

18

1. Joanna Southcott
Joanna Southcott/Southcote (1750–1814) was a self-described religious prophetess from Devon, England. Originally a member of the Church of England, she joined the Wesleyans around 1792. A 'Southcottian' movement continued in various forms after her death. Persuaded that she possessed supernatural gifts, Southcott wrote and dictated prophecies in rhyme, and then announced herself as the Woman of the Apocalypse spoken of in a prophetic passage of the Revelation (12:1–6).

1. John Dillinger

John Herbert Dillinger (1903–1934) was an American gangster active during the Great Depression. He operated with a group of men known as the 'Dillinger Gang' or 'The Terror Gang' which was accused of robbing twenty-four banks and four police stations, among other crimes. Dillinger escaped from jail twice. He was one of the first twentieth-century organized crime figures to court publicity and the media ran exaggerated accounts of his bravado and colourful personality, styling him as a Robin Hood figure for his era. The Dillinger gang was the catalyst for the FBI's development of more sophisticated investigative techniques in the battle against organized crime. In July 1934 the police tried to arrest Dillinger as he exited a theatre in Chicago and he was shot dead in the gun-battle that followed.

20

1. Seanchán Torpéist

Senchán/Seanchán Torpéist (sixth–seventh century AD) was the Chief Poet of Connacht in 598 when he succeeded Dallán Forgaill as Chief Ollam of Ireland. He is said to have been descended from the Munster-based Araidh sept based on the border between north Tipperary and Limerick.

From the late ninth century onwards, various tales portray Senchán as chief poet of his era in addition to being an arrogant and demanding figure. He is closely associated with Guaire Aidni, King of Connacht, and is credited with compiling the earliest prototype of the Gaelic epic, the Táin Bó Cuailnge, thereby rescuing it from oblivion. Geoffrey Keating's 'History of Ireland' states that Senchán ('Seanchán mac Cuairfheartaigh') was appointed Chief Ollam over Connacht at the Synod or Convention of Drumceat in 584 AD. Some of Senchán's writings are preserved in *The (Great) Book of Lecan (Leabhar (Mór) Leacáin)*.

2. Táin Bó Cuailnge

The Táin Bó Cuailnge (The Cattle Raid of Cooley or The Táin), an epic from early Irish literature, is frequently classed as the 'The Irish Iliad'. A legendary tale that has inspired the work of many renowned artists and writers in succeeding centuries, The Táin is traditionally set in the first century or the pre-Christian heroic age and is the central text in a body of tales known as the Ulster Cycle. The epic recounts a war against Ulster by Queen Medb of Connacht and her husband King Ailill. A central aspect of the attempted invasion of Ulster was a raid with the intention of stealing the highly prized stud bull of Cooley known as Donn Cuailnge. The primary opposition to the invaders was provided by the young warrior-demigod Cú Chulainn.

3. *Dochartach Duibhlionna agus Scéalta Eile; Ar an Tráigh Fhoilimh; Creach Chuinn Uí Dhomhnaill; Séamus Mac Murchaidh*

Various prose and poetry works produced by Seosamh Mac Grianna during the early years of his writing career, based on traditional Gaelic sources and lore from his home region around Donegal. *Dochartach Duibhlionna agus Scéalta Eile* was a collection of short stories, rooted in the oral tradition, which he published in 1936.

4. Pádraic Ó Conaire

From Galway city originally, Pádraic Ó Conaire (1882–1928) wrote primarily in the Irish language. One of the earliest writers of modernist fiction in the Irish language, he was incredibly prolific over the course of his short life, producing 26 books, 473 stories, 237 essays and 6 plays. He is best known for his acclaimed novel *Deoraíocht* (*Exile*) set amongst the Irish diaspora community in England. Ó Conaire emigrated to London in 1899 where he secured a civil service job in Britain's Board of Education. Ó Conaire was a central, pioneering figure in the Gaelic Revival of the late 1800s that witnessed a renewed interest in the Irish language and Gaelic culture. Alongside Patrick Pearse, Ó Conaire is regarded as one of the most important Irish-language short story writers of the early twentieth century.

5. Liam O'Flaherty (Liam Ó Flaithearta)

From the Irish-speaking Aran Islands off the coast of Galway originally, Liam O'Flaherty (1896–1984) was a major twentieth-century Irish novelist and short story writer whose primary output was in English, although he wrote in both Irish and English. O'Flaherty joined the British Army and fought on the Western Front in the First World War where he suffered severe injuries in 1917. Following the war, O'Flaherty was a founding member of the Communist Party of Ireland.

TRANSLATOR'S NOTE

It was a privilege to translate *Mo Bhealach Féin* (*This Road of Mine*) and to ensure that this unique work and its creator, Seosamh Mac Grianna, receive both a wider audience and the recognition that is their due.

Vast cultural swathes of the world, particularly on the Asian continent, remain 'untranslated' and unknown to the rest of the world, and ironically the same is true of the Irish-language tradition, from which less than a handful of books have been translated as of yet. Compounding this irony is the fact that while new technologies have ensured that the world has never been so 'small', true and meaningful dialogue and understanding remains at a premium and there are many who would argue that the culture of 'spin' has become an art-form in itself. In a society where information (and indeed misinformation) is manipulated and 'managed', the question of truth and its interpretation has re-emerged as one of the crucial philosophical questions of our day. As with the work of Orwell, Mac Grianna's musings on the nature of truth in *This Road of Mine* display a sense of foresight that is as strange as it is powerful.

It is a truism to say that literary translation helps us to engage with the world and to shape our understanding of it in new and essential ways. It is a truism that bears repetition nonetheless. And nowhere is translation more essential than in the case of a postcolonial country on the outermost margins of Europe such as Ireland, a relatively young nation historically speaking and one where two very different languages and cultures have co-existed for centuries but where for a complexity of reasons – economic, historical and cultural – the Anglophone world long ago assumed dominance.

Of all the twentieth-century Irish-language writers who carved out a radical new idiom in the language alongside the emergence of the new, urbanized Irish state, Mac Grianna was the most successful at fusing the oral Gaelic tradition stretching back thousands of years with a modernist literary perspective. He was clearly a very cultured man and aware of all the literary and artistic movements and concerns of his day as indicated by his personal interest in painting and the appearance of absurdist tropes, amongst others, in his text. Mac Grianna was intrigued by outsiders and his fascination with anyone who challenged the status quo resonates as powerfully as ever in present-day culture. He merged such themes with aspects of Irish culture that have been elided over time but that continually re-surface in the narrative. To take just one example: as apparently a straightforward and innocuous a term as 'leath-chairde' (casual friends) is redolent of the older Celtic or Gaelic culture and its hierarchical layers of friendship or kinship, the significance of which has long disappeared in Ireland.

Of much interest also is Mac Grianna's re-engagement with characters from our Gaelic past, and people and places of enormous significance for Irish people in generations gone by. In *This Road of Mine* Mac Grianna breathes new life into aspects of our culture that have remained dormant for far too long – Parthalán, the Churl of the Grey Coat, Macha Mongrua and the Táin to name but a few – and gives them a powerful new impetus and relevance.

When great literature is discussed nowadays in the Anglophone sphere, people inevitably cite Shakespeare, Joyce, Dickens, Wilde, Twain, etc. The English language has never had a monopoly on great writing however, as witnessed by literary figures as diverse as Homer, Dante, Proust, Cervantes, Tolstoy, Chekhov and Dostoyevsky, all of whom wrote in healthy languages with large populations of speakers. Seosamh Mac Grianna, a writer in what was even then the native language of a very small minority – the oldest written vernacular in Europe – is another name that can now be added to this pantheon. *This Road of Mine* is illusive in the best possible sense of the term. What appears on the surface as a relatively slim book describing a harsh but straightforward journey by foot along the roads of England and Wales, complete with the clearest of signposts and markers, proves multi-layered, and is really an inner journey of the mind where the artist questions the nature of creativity, truth and the meaning of life and art. And this is topped off in a prose that is sparse and beautiful in its simplicity, and a language that is highly poetic. I strove to convey the flavour of this in English, while remaining faithful to the Irish text as completely as possible, but without following to the letter all original layout such as paragraph breaks.

*

As regards my translation work, I have been granted the opportunity to translate the innermost thoughts of the two most imaginative souls who wrote in Irish in the twentieth century, both north and south – Seosamh Mac Grianna and Seán Ó Ríordáin – and for this, I am very grateful. I would like to thank Seosamh Ó Murchú for his encouragement and support and Bridget Farrell for her excellent editorial eye.

M. Ó hAodha, July 2020